RIDING HARD

DIRTY RYDERS MC SERIES BOOK 1

K.L. RAMSEY

Riding Hard (Dirty Riders MC Series Book 1)

Copyright © 2023 by K.L. Ramsey

Cover Design: Coffin Print Designs

Formatting: Mr. K.L.

Imprint:Independently published

First Print Edition: November 2023

All rights reserved.

No part of this book may be reproduced, scanned, or distributed in any printed or electronic form without permission. Please do not participate in or encourage piracy of copyrighted materials in violation of the author's rights. Thank you for respecting the hard work of this author.

This is a work of fiction. Names, characters, places, and incidents either are the product of the author's imagination or are used fictitiously, and any resemblance to locales, events, business establishments, or actual persons—living or dead—is entirely coincidental.

OWEN

Owen Blaine wasn't about to let the sexy red head in the corner go home with anyone else except him. She was the hottest woman he'd seen in a damn long time and the way the other guys seemed to be circling her just plain pissed him off. Even his older brother, Maverick was eyeing her and if he let his brother get to her first, there would be no doubt that Mav would be the one she'd be leaving with tonight. He couldn't let that happen. The last time he and his brother were involved with the same woman, they both ended up heart-broken, not that Mav ever let on that he was.

"Who's the hot chick in the corner?" Maverick asked.

"No idea," Owen admitted. She hadn't ever been into the Dirty Riders club before. He would have remembered her if she had. "She's not that hot," he lied, trying to throw his brother off her scent. From the hungry look in his eyes, Mav wasn't buying what he was selling.

"You're a fucking liar," Mav accused. "I saw the way that you looked at her. Hell, every guy in this fucking place is looking at her. You going to do something about it or is she up for grabs?"

"Up for grabs," Owen repeated. "Jesus, Mav, you're an asshole, aren't you?"

His brother threw back his head and laughed at what Owen had said and he blew out his breath. It could have gone either way with his brother. Either he'd say something that would have Mav pounding on his face or he'd just laugh. Owen was glad that his brother thought that he was being funny because he didn't have time for stitches tonight.

"Thanks, man," Maverick said. "So, you gonna go over there and talk to her, or am I? After the deal with both of us dating Amy, I don't want to have to deal with any of that shit again. You followed her around like a fucking puppy."

"Did not," Owen shouted over the music. "You're an asshole and I'm going over there and talking to her."

"All right then," Mav said. "When you strike out, let me know so that I can beat these other fuckers to her."

"I'm not going to strike out," Owen insisted. Sure, he probably would, but he was trying to stay positive, even if his brother was most likely going to win the girl. It's how things usually went when they wanted the same girl. Hell, they even fought over girls back in high school, not that any of them ever paid attention to Owen once Maverick or his twin, Steel, walked into the room. His older twin brothers always got the girls, and he was getting sick of playing second fiddle to them both.

When they weren't fighting over a woman, things were usually pretty good between them. It had been just the three of them for so long, that Owen had forgotten how life was when their parents were still around. His dad left when he was just a little kid and for a long time, it was just him, Mav, Steel, and

Riding Hard

their mom. She got cancer when he was a junior in high school and died before he graduated, but Maverick and Steel were there to watch him walk across the stage. They even got him a cake and threw him a little party—just the three of them, to celebrate. Maverick and Steel had become his only family and the three of them had learned how to get along in life together.

Steel joined the Navy at about the same time as Owen had joined the Army. He was a medic and had served two deployments so far. He knew that them both taking off on Maverick wasn't fair, but he insisted that they follow their own paths. Maverick stayed in town, opening his own bike shop, and whenever Owen and Steel could get home for a visit, they did. The one thing Owen was sure of—if he needed one of his older brothers, they'd be there for him, no questions asked.

He knew that Mav was right—if he didn't go over and ask the pretty woman out, one of the other guys would, and then, he'd miss out on his chance with her. Owen walked across the bar to where she sat and stared her down. He was willing her to turn around and notice him, but she just kept her eyes on her beer that she had been nursing. He cleared his throat twice before she turned to look over her shoulder at him.

"Can I help you?" she asked. God, he hoped so.

"Um, I saw you sitting here alone and thought that you might let me buy you a drink," he said.

The woman held up her beer and shook her head. "I already have one," she said. "I'm good." She was blowing him off and sure, that was like a kick in the nuts—especially when he looked over to find his older brother laughing at him. There was no way that he was going to give Maverick his chance with her. Not without a fight.

Owen sat down on the barstool next to her and she sighed,

3

picked up her beer and purse from the bar top, and slid down one stool. Ouch—that hurt, but he wasn't about to let it deter him. Even with Mav's laughter playing like a record skipping on a record player behind him, he felt some crazy determination to get to know this woman.

"My name's Owen," he said.

"Well, Owen, I'd say that it's nice to meet you, but that would be a lie. I thought that you'd take the hit to get lost when I turned your drink offer down," she said.

"I was just trying to be friendly," he breathed. "Won't happen again." The woman nodded and chugged down the last half of her beer. She pulled a ten from her purse and tossed it onto the bar, thanking the bartender, Spade, for the beer and even smiling at the guy. What the fuck?

Owen watched as the pretty woman walked back to the bathroom and disappeared through the door. "You fucking struck out, didn't you?" Maverick taunted. He sat down on the stool that the pretty little red head had just vacated and smiled over at him. "You can buy me a beer if it will make you feel better," Maverick teased.

"You can go fuck yourself," Owen said under his breath, just loud enough that he knew his brother heard him. His laughter rang out through the bar, garnering them more attention than Owen was hoping for.

"Can you shut the fuck up?" Owen grumbled. "I don't need every guy in here knowing that I struck out with her."

"Agreed," Maverick said, sobering, "I don't need the competition when I ask her out. Not that any of these assholes are my competition or anything." Maverick mean mugged a few of the guys who were hanging back by the ladies' room door, waiting for the pretty red head to come out.

Riding Hard

"Looks like you're going to have some competition whether you think they are or not," Owen taunted.

"Yeah, I'm going to have to knock some skulls together," he said. Maverick stood just as a woman's scream rang out from the ladies' room. "What the fuck?" he asked. Owen was about to ask the same thing, but his brother beat him to it. He had a sick feeling that the sexy red head was in trouble because he hadn't seen any women go back there in a while. Hell, there weren't a lot of women at the bar tonight. That's why the guys were salivating over the hot red head.

He followed close behind Maverick as they made their way through the crowd of guys who were trying to get a glimpse of what was going on. Mav pushed his way through the ladies' room door, not bothering to knock, to find the sexy red head on the floor, blood trickling down from her forehead.

"Don't move her," Owen ordered. His Army medic training was kicking in and it helped that he rode for the local ambulance services on weekends to earn some extra cash. "Call 911," he shouted back to Spade.

"On it," Spade shouted.

"Give me your jacket," Owen ordered. Maverick immediately removed his leather jacket and handed it over to him. "Thanks," he murmured as he balled it up and put it under the woman's head.

"Who would have done this?" Maverick asked. Owen looked around the room to find the guys watching them and shook his head.

"I'm not sure," Owen said. "I didn't see anyone follow her in." He had been watching too. He didn't take his eyes off the door after the sexy red head disappeared into the bathroom. He looked around the small room and noticed that the bathroom window was open and was big enough to possibly fit a person through it—a smaller person, not one of the hulking guys standing around them.

"Her purse is missing," Owen said, looking around. "She picked it up, paid her bar tab, and then walked back here to the bathroom. Did someone knock her out just to rob her?"

"Don't know, but I think that we should look around outside, just in case someone used that window to escape," Mav said, as if reading Owen's earlier thoughts.

"Agreed. I'll stay here with her, and you take a couple of guys you can trust to look around outside," Owen ordered. When it came to things like this, Maverick usually let him take the lead. It was his military training that had gotten them both out of a good deal of scrapes. Owen was used to calling the shots when the odds were against him and from the way things looked for the pretty red head, she'd need someone to call the shots until she could get back on her feet. He might be crazy for thinking about doing it, but he was going to stick by her until she told him to get lost again. It was the least he could do for the pretty woman who blew him off at the bar and if it won him brownie points, he'd take them.

TILLY

Matilda Newton wasn't sure how she had ended up at a biker bar, surrounded by big, bearded, tattooed men who didn't want to seem to take no for an answer. She was determined to try to put her bad day behind her and find a way out of the mess she had gotten herself into. She just never imagined that the little dive bar she picked to hide away, and think, would be a biker bar.

She sat in the corner hoping that everyone would leave her alone, but being one of the only single women in the place garnered her some unwanted attention that she couldn't seem to shake. When she had to spell it out for the hot biker that she wasn't interested in him buying her a beer, he seemed a bit hurt. That wasn't Tilly's intention, but she had already politely turned him down once. She just wanted to be left alone until she could figure out what to do with the hard drive that she had swiped off her boss's desk. Apparently, it was important enough to Nate that he called her about twenty-five times since she had left the office, threatening to come after her if she didn't give it back to him. His threats grew darker and more menacing and the messages longer as time passed, and she worried that he'd make good on every one of them if she didn't give the drive back to him.

She knew that Nate was doing something illegal, and now, she was sure of it. Tilly was also sure that the information that she'd need to bring him down was on the hard drive that he kept under lock and key in his desk. He was foolish enough to leave the key on the desk when he ran to lunch and Tilly snooped, against her better judgment. Now, she had her boss and who knew who else chasing after her and the one thing she was sure of was she couldn't go home. She was sure that if she did, she'd find Nate waiting for her there and he'd be ready to make good on his threats.

Her only hope at getting out of there was going to be to pay her tab, tell they biker sitting next to her to fuck off, and regroup in the bathroom. Then, she'd be able to figure out where to go next and who she could trust. Honestly, she had no one to turn to, and that made her feel desperate and alone. She almost wanted to take the biker up on his offer of a drink and then, ask him to take her someplace safe, but that would give him the wrong idea. She needed a safe place to land that didn't involve his bed for the night because she was sure that would be what he wanted in return for helping her out.

She spent about five minutes in the mirror, trying to talk herself into going home with the sexy biker when a shadow in the corner caught her eye. It was a man—at least she thought it was. He had a slight build, and she was sure that he had gotten in through the window somehow.

Riding Hard

"I don't want to hurt you," he breathed as he stepped out of the shadows. "I just want the drive," he said.

"Nate," she breathed. "How did you get in here? How did you know that I was here?"

"I knew that sooner or later, you'd get up to no good and do some snooping, so I put a tracker on your car. I saw you sitting at the bar drinking and assumed that at some point, you'd need to use the ladies' room, so I climbed in through the window."

"You've been tracking me?" she spat. She knew that he was a weasel, but she had no idea that he's stoop to such lows.

"Yes, and now, all I want is the hard drive," he said, stepping toward her with his hand out.

"I don't have it. I ditched it someplace for safe keeping on my way here," she lied.

His smile was mean, "You do know that I can trace your path here, right? You didn't make any stops, which means it's on you or in that purse you're clutching for dear life." He nodded to her purse, and she hugged it to her chest.

"You can't take this," she said. "It has sentimental value," she lied. She had just purchased it on a whim about two weeks ago.

"Again, with the lies," he tisked. "You really are the worst liar, Tilly. Just give me the fucking drive and this can all be over."

"If you come one step closer, I'll scream. There are a lot of big, bad ass bikers out there and I'm sure that they'll come in here to my rescue. One even asked to buy me a drink, so I'm sure that you won't be able to just leave here unscathed." She wasn't sure of anything, but she was hoping that was what would end up happening. Hell, for all she knew, the sexy-as-sin biker had given up on her and left while she was in the bathroom.

"Go ahead and scream, Tilly," he said. "I'll have what I want from you and be out of here before they can even find your body." He took another step in her direction, pulling a gun from his jacket pocket. Tilly couldn't help the screech that escaped her lips. She let it out with all her might and when he realized what had happened, Nate hit her in the temple with the butt of the gun, knocking her to the ground. The last thing Tilly remembered as her world went dark was Nate taking her purse out of her hands as he laughed at her.

"Should have just given me the fucking hard drive, Tilly," he breathed on his way out of the bathroom window. Nate disappeared into the night as she closed her eyes, giving into the darkness.

Tilly woke up to two men arguing about who was going to get to keep her and she knew that had to be wrong. Why would anyone be arguing about who was going to get to keep her? She opened her eyes and groaned as they adjusted to the light. Her head was throbbing, and she was sure that had everything to do with her boss hitting her with the handle of his gun. It could have been worse—he could have used the gun correctly and shot her. She was thankful that wasn't the case.

"Where am I?" she asked blinking up at the two men who were standing over her.

"Take it easy—you're in the hospital." She looked up at the man standing over her and recognized him from the bar.

"You were the guy I turned down at the bar," she whispered. Her voice sounded hoarse, and she tried to sit up. "Can I get some water?" The guy standing on the other side of her laughed and helped her take a sip of the water cup that was sitting on the table next to him.

Riding Hard

"I'm not the guy you turned down," he said. "You turned down my little brother there though, so I'd say that your memory is working just fine." She hadn't turned the big, grizzly-looking guy down, but she would have. He was bigger than his brother and covered in tattoos. He wasn't bad looking at all, but just not her type. She liked the guys she went out with a little cleaner cut. In fact, the one she turned down was her type, not that she'd admit that to either of them.

"Can you please tell me where I am?" she asked again.

"You're in the hospital, and I'm Owen Blaine. That's my brother, Maverick. You were knocked out in the ladies' room at the bar we were at. I think someone stole your purse too." Yeah, she remembered exactly who took her purse, but that wasn't something she was going to share with either of them. She'd save that for the police, as soon as she was up to going to the station to file a report.

"Well, I appreciate you getting me to the hospital, but I think that I can take it from here," she said, sitting up. She immediately had to lie back down. She felt nauseous and dizzy. "The room is spinning."

"You have a concussion and can't get up," Owen warned. "You'll need to stay here over night," he added.

"I can't do that," she said. "He'll find me here and finish what he started." The thought of Nate finding her in the hospital and actually using the gun he had, to kill her, scared the hell out of her.

"Who will?" Maverick asked.

"My boss," she almost whispered, "he did this to me. He had a gun."

"Why would your boss want to hurt you?" Owen asked.

"That is a long story, and my head is killing me," she whispered. The less they knew, the better. She was going to have to figure out how to handle Nate on her own because dragging strangers into her mess wouldn't be fair to either of them.

"I'll stay with you tonight," Owen offered. "That way, you can get some rest and not have to worry about your boss getting in here."

"You don't have to do that," she insisted.

"Well, I wasn't asking, I was letting you know that I'll be right here for the night. Then, when you get discharged, you're coming home with me," he said.

"Oh, I can't do that," she breathed. "I don't even know you."

"Sure you do—I'm the guy from the bar who you turned down. You can't go back to your place. I'm betting your boss knows where you live," he said.

"Good point," she said.

"He's right, you can't go back to your place. So, you need to decide—are you going home with Owen or me?" Maverick asked, puffing out his chest, making her giggle. Tilly groaned and grabbed her head. "Sorry, didn't mean to make it worse," he said.

"You didn't," she said, "they say laughter is the best medicine. Listen, you guys can't just take me in. I don't want to be anyone's problem and if you get involved in this, you'll be in over your heads, just like I am."

"How about you let us decide what we will and won't be involved in? We want to help you out," Owen said.

"Well, I will need a place to lay low for a bit, until I can figure out what to do about Nate," she said.

"Nate?" Maverick asked.

"Yeah, he's my boss—the one who knocked me out," she said. The thought of going back to her place scared the hell out of her

Riding Hard

and Nate didn't know either of the big bikers standing by her bedside. If she went home with one of them, she'd be able to take her time to figure out her next move.

OWEN

Owen felt as though he was holding his breath waiting for the pretty red head to answer Maverick's question. "Um, we don't even know your name," he breathed.

"That's another good reason why neither of you should take me home with you. It's Matilda, by the way, but everyone calls me Tilly."

"That's an unusual name," Maverick said.

"Oh?" Tilly questioned, "and, Maverick is so normal?" Owen had to admit, he really liked that this woman seemed to like to give his older brother shit as much as he did.

"Good point," Mav breathed.

"Well, I was named after my grandmother and everyone called her Matilda, so I guess I got stuck with Tilly. I don't mind, really. I don't know anyone else with my name. I got her red hair and her name. She was really a wonderful person, so, I'd say that I'm lucky."

Riding Hard

"I was named after my grandfather," Owen said. "My mom wanted to name one of my brothers after him, but they were twins, and she didn't want to give one a special family name and not the other. So, she waited to give it to me."

"Yeah, yeah," Maverick grumbled, "you're very special. Now, can you please decide who you will be going home with?" He stared Tilly down and she sighed.

"Owen," she breathed. "I'd go stay with my sister, but she has a toddler, and my boss knows where she lives too. In fact, I need to make sure that she's okay."

"Oh, well, I'm honored," he said feeling quite victorious.

"Don't be," Tilly warned. "You seem to be the lesser of two evils. Honestly, I just Eeny, meeny, miny, moed in my head and you won." He didn't feel like a winner after her admission.

"Um, thanks," Owen mumbled.

"Well, on that note, I'm going to hit the road." Maverick was going to go home and pout, Owen just knew it. That's usually how things played out when he didn't get his way—he sulked. "The cops were here earlier to check in on you and said that they'd be back here later," Mav said. "Have Owen text me your sister's address and I'll stop by to check on her and let her know that you're in the hospital. I'm betting she hasn't gotten word yet."

"Thanks for letting me know. I appreciate you stopping by Melody's place to let her know what happened to me. I'm going to get some rest until the cops get here," Tilly said. Her eyes were closed before Maverick even made it to the door. Owen knew that she had to be in pain and rest would be the best thing for her.

He followed Maverick into the hallway and made sure that the door was closed before stopping his brother from getting

15

onto the elevator. "You really going to stop by her sister's place to check in on her and let her know what happened to Tilly?"

"Yep," Mav said. His brother usually resorted to one-syllable words when he was pissed off.

"Don't be a sore loser," Owen said.

"I'm not a fucking sore loser," Maverick said. He sighed as if realizing that he sounded exactly like a sore loser. "Listen, I have to get up early to head to work." His brother owned a bike shop and was one of the best mechanics that Owen knew and when their mother died, he started up his own shop to help bring in some extra cash to help pay the bills their mom left behind. Steel had already joined the Navy, shortly after their mother passed, and Maverick took care of Owen and things back at home. His brother never complained about not being able to take off and do what he wanted. He took responsibility for Owen and got him through his last year of high school. If there was one thing that Owen knew it was that he could always count on his big brother. Mav was one of a kind.

"I didn't mean it, man," Owen said. "Listen, thanks for checking in on Tilly's sister. Will you text me to let me know that she's okay? I'll let Tilly know."

"And you'll be able to play the hero, delivering the good news?" Maverick asked.

"It's not like that," Owen said.

"Are you still claiming that you don't like her?" Mav asked.

"No," Owen said, "yes," he corrected. "Fuck, I don't know. I just know that I feel bad for what happened to her, and I want to help her. I'm not trying to play the hero."

"If you say so," Maverick grumbled, stepping onto the elevator after the doors opened. "I'll be in touch." His brother smirked as he waved back at him as the doors closed. Owen

Riding Hard

grumbled that his older brother was an ass as he walked back into the room to find Tilly sound asleep. He hated doing it, but he needed her sister's information to text Maverick. Then, he planned on letting her get some rest while he filled in the cops about her asshole boss being the one who attacked her at the bar. Maybe they'd be able to put the fucker in jail and Tilly would actually be able to relax and recover.

"Tilly," he whispered. She moaned and rolled away from him. "Tilly, I need your sister's information." She grumbled something about him being persistent and honestly, she had no idea how persistent he could be.

"I'm sorry that I have to wake you, but Maverick just left and wants to stop by your sister's place on his way home," Owen explained.

"Oh, that's nice of him," she said. She rambled off her sister's information as he texted it to Mav.

"He has his moments, but my brother's a good guy. I'm sure that he'll check in on your sister and let her know what's happening with you," Owen assured.

"Well, I appreciate both of you helping me out. I'm sorry that you have to do all of this for me just because my boss decided to be a jerk," she said.

"I wouldn't call robbing you in the ladies' room and giving you a concussion, him being a jerk," Owen said. "Why would he do that to you anyway? What was in that purse that he had to knock you out to take it from you?"

"It's a long story," she said.

"Well, if you're up to telling it, I have nowhere to go," Owen said. He sat down in the chair next to her bedside and waited her out.

"I work for an investment firm and Nate is my boss. I'm his

personal assistant and well, I knew he was up to no good, I just had no idea what it was. That's why I took the hard drive off his desk and shoved it into my purse. I was sitting at the bar tonight trying to figure out my next move—you know, what I should do with the hard drive and if I should question my boss directly. I guess I got my answer when I found him standing in the ladies' room."

"Do you know what was on the hard drive?" Owen asked. It had to be pretty bad if the guy was willing to steal it back and hurt his assistant in the process.

"I didn't get a chance to look at it," she admitted. "I was sitting at that bar, trying to figure out what to do with the hard drive when you asked to buy me a drink," she said. "I wasn't sure if I should turn it over to the police without knowing what was on it. Honestly, I was going to go home and look at it when I got done in the bathroom, but Nate found me in there. He said that he knew that sooner or later, I'd figure it all out and he put a tracker on my car."

"I'll have Mav run over to look at your car and remove the tracker," he offered. "He owns an auto body shop and I'm sure that he won't mind keeping it there for the time being."

"I appreciate that," she said. "You both are going to a lot of trouble for someone you don't really know. I won't ever be able to pay either of you back."

"There is no need to pay us back. Listen, we're not here for paybacks, thanks, or anything else. We just want to help you out. Your boss sounds like an ass and bringing him down will be enough thanks for both of us."

"I'm sure that you have a job to go to and a life to get back to," she insisted. Yeah, it felt as though she was giving him the brush off again, and that hurt a bit, but he wasn't about to let her push him away—not when she was in danger.

"You don't know this about me, but I'm in the security business," he admitted. Once Owen got out of the Army, he came home and tried to figure out his next step in life. He struggled for a while, even thinking about going to medical school, but his heart just wasn't in it. Maverick and Steel sat him down and talked to him about having to make some hard and fast decisions because there was no way that either of them was going to let him just sit around and rot. That's when he decided to start his own business. He started a security firm and honestly, he was surprised at how many clients he had. He even had to turn some away.

"Um, I hate to tell you this, but I'm broke, and now, I'm pretty sure that I'm out of a job. I would never be able to hire you, Owen," she said.

"Well, I wasn't asking you to pay me," he said. "I want to help you and I can. Sometimes, it's okay to let people help you out in life without giving them anything in return," Owen said.

"You wouldn't expect anything from me?" she asked. Tilly stared him down and he could tell exactly what she was thinking. He had hit on her just hours ago, at the bar. Why wouldn't she think he was doing this because he wanted to get into her pants?

"Nothing," he said firmly. "I know that I asked to buy you a beer, but our relationship going forward will be strictly professional. I'll be your security guard and you'll be my client."

"I can't exactly be your client if I'm not paying you to do the job, Owen," she insisted.

"Fine, my fee is twenty dollars. Do you have twenty dollars, Tilly?" he asked.

"Um, I do," she said.

"Great, then, you have yourself a bodyguard." The thought of guarding her body made him hot, but there was no way that he'd tell her that. For now, he'd keep his promise to keep her safe, because he had a feeling that her asshole boss wasn't going to stop coming for Tilly, even if she had no idea what he wanted from her.

TILLY

Tilly woke from a dead sleep and looked around, trying to figure out where she was. "Oh, yeah—the hospital," she croaked. She tried to sit up and groaned when her head started throbbing again.

"Your cell phone has been going crazy," Owen said. He was still sitting in the uncomfortable-looking chair next to her bed. A part of her wanted to ask him why he was still hanging around, but then she remembered that he had agreed to be her security guard—as if she needed one. Honestly, the more time that passed without Nate showing up at the hospital, the sillier she felt. What if this whole thing was just a giant misunderstanding? What if she was blowing things out of proportion and her boss wasn't really up to no good? That was a lot of what-ifs, even for her.

Tilly was always good at second-guessing herself. Ever since she was a kid, she was constantly making a decision and then, changing her mind. The problem was, that she never felt good enough to make the right decisions, even in her own life.

"It must be my sister," she said, "she's the only one who really calls my phone. Well, her and Nate, but I'm guessing that he's not going to call me again."

"Yeah, I don't think that's going to happen, especially since I'm planning on having the guy put in jail for what he did to you. The cops are coming by this morning and will want to talk to you if you're up to it," he said.

"I'm ready to talk to them. I just want this nightmare to be over. Will I be able to leave the hospital today?" she asked.

"They said that I should be able to take you home later today if you pass all the tests," he said.

"Tests," she squeaked, "what kind of tests?"

"Don't worry, you didn't have to study for them or anything," Owen teased. Even rolling her eyes at him made her head hurt, but it was worth the smile he gave her.

"Good to know," she grumbled. "Can you hand me my phone so that I can call my sister? I'm sure that Melody has a bunch of questions to ask me, and I'd like to get that part over with. Then, I'm sure she'll slide into the whole, 'I told you so' speech before we end the call."

"Why would she say that?" he asked.

"Because she warned me not to take the job. She met Nate and said that he was giving her vibes," she said. "Which usually means that the guy's a jerk. She was right, he was a jerk."

"He's more than a jerk, Tilly," Owen said. "He's a criminal." She nodded, knowing that what he was saying was true, but still not wanting to admit it out loud yet.

"Would you mind giving me a little bit of privacy while I call my sister?" she asked. The hurt flashed across his face, and she

Riding Hard

almost wanted to take her request back, but she didn't really know Owen, and telling her sister about what had happened to her was going to be hard enough.

"Sure," he said, "if that's what you want." He walked out of the small hospital room and all she could do was watch him go.

Tilly sighed and concentrated on finding her sister's number in her contacts. It was hard to focus with her throbbing head, but she found it and when her sister answered, she couldn't help but burst into tears.

"What's wrong, Tilly?" Melody asked. "Are you okay? Did the doctors give you bad news?"

"No, it's just good to hear your voice," Tilly admitted.

"It's good to hear your voice too," Melody said. "I've been so worried since you sent that big biker over here to tell me about your accident."

"It wasn't an accident. In fact, I think that it was done on purpose. You were right about my boss, Melody. He's a slime ball and he's up to no good."

"And now, you're wrapped up in his mess, aren't you?" her sister asked. "I know you, sis, you can't seem to keep your nose out of trouble. Tell me that you didn't get mixed up in the middle of his mess."

"I wish I could," Tilly grumbled, "but, I can't. I found a hard drive on his desk and knew that I had to take my chance and grab it while he was out. I slipped it into my purse and left the office. I had no idea that Nate was tracking my car or that he'd follow me to the biker bar where I went to hide away in. I thought that he'd never look at a place like that for me."

"Well, I don't think that anyone would look for you in a biker bar. It's not really your typical hangout," Melody said.

"Yeah, well, he followed me there and when I went to the

ladies' room, he was waiting for me there. He climbed in through the window and left that way too, after he took my purse and knocked me out."

"That's awful," Melody murmured, "I'd like just five minutes with that asshole."

"It wouldn't do you any good," Tilly admitted. "Do you think he wouldn't do the same to you that he's done to me? June needs her mother." Her sister's two-year-old was Melody's whole world. She loved June with her whole heart and honestly, Tilly thought that was the only reason why her sister stayed with her loser husband. Adam was an abusive asshole, but her sister always explained away his behavior, saying that he had a bad day or that he was just going through a bad time. Tilly didn't buy all of Melody's excuses, no matter how convincing her sister was. She tried to keep her nose out of her sister's trouble, but it was getting harder to do lately.

"So, the biker you sent here, you know him well?" Melody asked.

"Um, no," Tilly squeaked. "I just met him and his brother at the biker bar that I went to. They want to help me though and honestly, I'm not sure where else to turn."

"You know, you can always come here," her sister offered. "I wouldn't let Nate anywhere near you."

"I appreciate that, sis, but I won't do that to you or June. Me coming to stay with you would only put you both in danger," Tilly said. "I'm going to stay with Owen. He owns a security firm, and he says that he can help me." She just hoped that he was being truthful and wasn't trying to get into her pants with his pretty promises.

"So, you're just going to stay with the big, burly biker?" Melody asked.

Riding Hard

"I think you're confusing Maverick and Owen," Tilly said. "Maverick is the one we sent over to check on you and tell you about what happened. His brother, Owen isn't as big or scary as his brother," Tilly said. "In fact, he's not scary at all," she whispered to herself.

"You like him," Melody accused.

"As I've already told you, I don't really know him. But he seems like a good guy, and I believe that he really wants to help me," Tilly said. Maybe she was setting herself up for disappointment, but she needed to be able to rely on someone. She was out of allies and having Owen on his side, and even his big, bad brother, Maverick, put her at ease.

"Well, his brother is scary as hell and honestly, he's annoying. He kept calling me 'Kid'," Melody said. "I mean, he's older than I am, but it was almost insulting." Tilly stifled her laugh, not wanting to piss off her sister.

"Maybe he was just trying to be respectful. I mean, you are a married woman with a child," Tilly reminded.

"Yeah, and if he called June, 'Kid,' that would feel normal, but I'm a grown woman," Melody said.

"I'm sure that he didn't mean anything by it," Tilly assured.

"Are you sure that you don't want to come stay here?" Melody asked. "Adam isn't really here that much these days. He is spending a lot of time at work. It would just be us girls."

"And that's exactly why I can't come over," Tilly said. "I won't put you and June in danger."

"Well, if you need me for anything, you'll call, right?" her sister asked.

"Of course," Tilly agreed. "I'll also keep you updated on everything. Hopefully, the cops will take my statement today and Nate will be behind bars, and I'll be able to move on from this horrible nightmare. If I get out of here today, I'll be at Owen's. I'll text you the address."

"Thanks," Melody said. "Stay safe, sis."

"You too," Tilly breathed and ended the call. She was going to talk to the police and then, she planned on begging the doctors and nurses to release her to go home—well, Owen's home, but anyplace had to be better than her little hospital room.

OWEN

Owen knew that giving Tilly the time and space that she needed was important in earning her trust, but he wanted to be by her side while she answered the cop's questions. Instead, they talked to the two of them separately, and by the time they finished, Tilly insisted that she wanted to be discharged, even though she looked completely worn out.

The nurses finally agreed to find a doctor to check Tilly out and possibly release her as Owen waited in the hallway for the final verdict. "How's she doing today?" Maverick asked, turning the corner from the elevators.

"What are you doing here?" Owen asked. He had a feeling that his brother had stopped by to see if Tilly had changed her mind about staying with him. Maverick didn't like to lose and stopping by the hospital was probably a skilled move in his plan to win over the pretty redhead.

"I just wanted to let you know that I stopped by Tilly's

sister's place to let her know what was going on," Mav said, running his hands through his overly-long hair. It was his telltale sign that he was up to no good.

"Yeah, Tilly told me that she got a call from her sister this morning about you showing up at her house. Thanks for doing that," Owen said.

"No problem," Mav breathed, "how's she doing?"

"About the same, but I think that they are going to release her today."

"And she's still going to stay with you?" Maverick asked.

"That's still the plan, why?" Owen questioned.

Mav held up his hands, wearing a shit-eating grin. "No reason," he insisted. "I was just making conversation."

"Well, cut it out," Owen said.

"If I'm being honest, I also stopped by to tell you that I talked to Mace and he's pretty pissed off that this happened at his club," Maverick said. Shit—the last thing Owen needed was to piss off their club's Prez. Mace was a good guy, but if he put you on his shit list, it was pretty hard to get off of it.

"I'll apologize to him and make things right," Owen said.

Mav barked out his laugh. "No, he's not mad at you. He's mad at Tilly's asshole boss for knocking her out while she was in his club. He wants the guy's head on a platter." Owen breathed out a sigh of relief knowing that Mace's anger wasn't geared toward him.

"Don't worry, man," Maverick said. "You're still a member of the Road Reapers."

"Thank God," Owen breathed. He had joined the Road Reapers shortly after Maverick and Steel did, a few years back. He loved that club with his whole heart. The guys in the club were like his brothers and he'd die for each and every one of

Riding Hard

them. They were a tight-knit group, and he wouldn't trade his club for anything.

"He'd like to talk to you and meet Tilly when she's up to it," Mav said.

"I'll bring her in this week if she feels like it. Thanks for relaying the message," Owen said.

"No problem," Maverick said.

"And thanks for running by Tilly's sister's place to tell her what happened," he said. Maverick groaned and he wondered if there was more to the story that he wasn't sharing. "You want to tell me what that noise is for?" he asked.

"Yeah—her sister was kind of a pain," he grumbled. "She's a kid and has a kid herself."

"A pain how?" Owen asked.

"She just seemed to be a bit of a know it all. You know how I can't stand women like that. Anyway, I told her about Tilly and then, we talked for a few minutes until her kid woke up." Owen couldn't help his smile. Mav really didn't understand kids. In fact, he avoided them as though they had the plague. A tiny baby crying was enough to send his brother over the edge and that fact had always amused Owen.

"So, the kid scared the hell out of you, right?" Owen asked.

"No, and shut the fuck up," Maverick grumbled.

"Yeah, okay," Owen said. "Well, I know that Tilly appreciates you risking life and limb to tell her sister and her sister's toddler about her accident."

"Shut the fuck up," Mav shouted, garnering some unwanted attention from the nurses around the corner.

"You're going to get us both thrown out of here, asshole," Owen loudly whispered.

"Excuse me, Mr. Blaine," a nurse said from behind him. Shit

—they were going to get kicked out of the hospital and then, who would take care of Tilly?

"Yes?" he asked, turning to face her while wearing his best smile.

"We're going to be releasing your girlfriend in about thirty minutes and need you to be ready to get your vehicle from the parking garage," she said. Maverick choked when the nurse called Tilly his girlfriend and he shout his brother a "Shut the fuck up" look.

"I'm ready whenever you are," Owen said, laying on the charm. "Thank you for letting me know. I'm sure that Tilly will be thrilled to get out of here." The nurse nodded and went back to the corner desk she and the other nurses shared.

"Girlfriend?" Maverick asked.

"Yeah, I had to tell them that we're together. Otherwise, they would have made me leave after visiting hours. By lying and saying that I'm her boyfriend, they let me stay the night with her —you know, to keep an eye out for her ex-boss."

"Right, to keep an eye out for her ex-boss. I'm sure that it has nothing to do with you being smitten by the redhead or wanting her to really be your girlfriend," Maverick teased.

"Shut the fuck up," Owen grumbled, giving him back his words. He was right though, not that he'd ever tell his brother that. He wanted Tilly and if lying and saying that he was her boyfriend meant that he wouldn't have to leave her side, then so be it.

"I have to run, but I'll check in with you in a couple of days. If you need me sooner, just call my cell," Maverick said.

"Thanks," Owen said. He was going to have to call on his brother sooner than he wanted because he was going to need to run some new security measures out at his place, but he'd bring

30

Riding Hard

all that up later. Right now, he wanted to get rid of his brother before Tilly was released. The last thing he wanted was his brother tagging along with the two of them when he showed her around his place and all but begged her to stay in his room with him.

He walked back into Tilly's hospital room, and she beamed up at him. "I get to go home," she said. "Well, not my home but I get to go home with you." Hearing her say that she was going home with him did strange things to his libido, but there was no way that he'd let her know that.

"I'm so happy that you're getting out of here," he said. "And I promise to make you feel at home in my home. It's just until we can make sure that you're safe."

"I know," she said, rolling her eyes at him. "I mean, I do have some memory issues, but I can remember what we talked about this morning." God, she was adorable. The past twenty-four hours together had shown him that he had good taste when it came to picking up women at the club. Sure, Tilly had turned him down flat, but he really liked the way things were turning in his favor. All it took was for poor Tilly to be attacked in the ladies' room at his club and need someone to take care of her. Yeah, that didn't make him sound like an asshole at all.

The nurse from the hallway walked into the room and smiled at Tilly. "Are you ready to get out of here?" she asked.

"I am," Tilly agreed. "And Owen has agreed to take good care of me."

The nurse smiled at him and nodded. "I'm sure that he will." He wasn't sure if the nurse really meant it or if she could secretly read his filthy mind and see just how he wanted to take care of Tilly. If that was the case, she wouldn't have let him anywhere near her patient.

"Um, I'll just go get my truck," he offered. "I'll meet you out front," he said.

"I'll be the one in a wheelchair," Tilly teased. He chuckled and walked out the door, hoping that he'd be able to get himself together on the walk to the parking garage. He needed to get his mind out of the gutter if he was going to be able to take care of Tilly and keep her safe. After all, that was what he promised to do for her.

TILLY

Tilly wasn't sure why she felt so nervous about going home with Owen, but she did. While the nurse was helping her get dressed, she kept calling Owen her "Boyfriend" and that made her both giddy and a ball of nerves.

"Do you live far away?" she asked. She honestly didn't even know where he lived. For all she knew, he was going to take her out to the middle of nowhere and leave her for dead. But then, why would he have gone through all the trouble to stay by her side for the past day that she was in the hospital? He would have dumped her off at the hospital and left her there—but he hadn't. Instead, he told the nurse that he was her boyfriend so that they'd let him stay the night with her. He had kept his promise and stayed by her side, making sure that Nate didn't get to her again to finish the job.

"Nope, just around the corner, really," Owen said. "We'll be there in just a few minutes."

"Oh, great," she said. "I guess I'm just a little bit more tired than I thought I was. Getting out of the hospital really took a toll on my energy levels."

"Well, as soon as we get to my place, I'll show you your room and you can take a nap," he offered.

"Are you sure?" she asked.

"Of course," he agreed. "I have a few things to do around the house and I'll make us some dinner."

"You cook?" she asked.

"Yes, I can cook," he said. Owen sounded a bit hurt by her question and she immediately regretted asking it.

"I didn't mean it that way," she insisted. "I was just surprised that's all. I mean, we met in a biker bar, and you don't scream "Chef" when I look at you. Plus, you've already told me that you're in security. I guess you're just naturally good at everything."

"Now, you're just trying to flatter me," he grumbled, causing her to giggle.

"Ouch," she said, grabbing her head. "I forgot how much it hurts to laugh with a concussion."

"Sorry," he said, "I'll try not to say anything that will make you laugh for the next few days."

"Thank you," she said.

"The doctors want me to wake you up every hour to check on you," he reminded. "If you want, you can stay in my room with me, to make it easier on both of us." She shot him a look and knew that she was going to turn him down before the words were even out of her mouth. How could she not? She didn't want him to get the wrong idea about everything if she climbed into his bed.

"Owen," she started, and he let out the breath that he was holding. Her tone sounded harsh to her own ears, and she knew

Riding Hard

that she wasn't going to hold back from telling him exactly how she felt about staying in his room with him. "I don't think that's a good idea. I mean, I appreciate you wanting to check on me, as the doctor ordered, but I'd prefer to stay on your sofa or something. I wouldn't even mind an air mattress." She was laying it on a bit thick. Tilly had made it clear that she'd rather sleep just about anywhere else rather than in his bed.

"Got it," he mumbled. "I think that I might have a ratty old mattress in my garage. Maybe you'd like to sleep on that?" he asked. He was being an ass, but she had brought on his attitude herself.

"Um, yeah," she reluctantly agreed. "If that's my only option, I'm good with it."

"Jesus, Tilly," he said. "You would really rather sleep anywhere except my bed, wouldn't you?" he asked.

"It's not that, Owen," she insisted. "I just don't want to give you the wrong idea about why I'm staying with you."

"No, I got that," he said. "You're staying with me so that I can keep you safe and make sure that your concussion doesn't get worse. I picked up on that as soon as you said the words, 'Air mattress,'" he said. "I was just hoping that you didn't still find me so repulsive." Repulsive was the last thing that she felt about Owen. Hot, bothered, and a whole lot turned on—all of that, but repulsed, not at all.

"You shouldn't put words in my mouth, Owen," she breathed. "I don't find you repulsive. I just don't think that it's a good idea for us to sleep in the same bed. If this is going to be a problem, I can find other accommodations." He pulled into what she assumed was his driveway and then, into the garage, shutting the door behind his truck.

"Come on, I'll show you to the air mattress," he said. He got out of the truck, and she wondered if she should follow him or demand that he take her some place else. He opened her door and helped her out, not giving her much of an option. Owen grabbed the bag that the hospital had given her with the clothes she was wearing from the night before. The nurses were kind enough to give her some scrubs to wear home and she was grateful that she didn't have to wear her blood-soaked outfit from the bar.

"This is the main floor. It's pretty standard—kitchen, family room, dining room, and stairs at the end of the hallway that goes up to the bedrooms." He emphasized the word, "Bedrooms" being plural, and she shot him a look. He was wearing his sexy smirk, and she couldn't help but smile back at him.

"You have more than one bedroom?" she asked, "and, you've let me worry about saying the wrong thing this whole time?"

"Yeah, but in my defense, my male ego was injured, and I needed a win. Plus, watching you squirm was pretty damn cute."

"Gee—thanks," she sassed.

"Come on, I'll show you to your bedroom. It is next door to mine, so I hope that's okay," he said. "I'll come in every hour to wake you up tonight and if you're good, then tomorrow, I won't have to do that anymore," Owen said, repeating the instructions that the nurse had given them before being discharged.

"Thank you, Owen," she said. "I appreciate you doing that for me, and if I'm being honest, I am glad that I don't have to sleep on an air mattress—or an old ratty mattress from your garage."

"Yeah, I wasn't really playing fair when I told you about that," he said. "I'd say that I was sorry, but you did make it pretty easy."

Riding Hard

"How about I take a nap and you'll be able to make fun of me all you want to later?" she asked.

"Deal," he agreed. "You need to rest up so that you can get better, Tilly."

"Right, then I can figure out what Nate is up to and what was on that hard drive," Tilly said. That was something that she wanted more than anything. That hard drive had nearly cost Tilly her life and it had cost her a job that she liked—not that she'd ever go back to Nate now.

"We can figure out what he's up to together," Owen insisted.

"I have a little bit of a confession," she admitted. While she was being questioned by the cops, one of the officers told her that even with her testimony, they might not be able to lock Nate away because he had some iron clad alibi. Her worst night-mare was possibly coming true—she had told the cops her story about what Evan had done to her, and he was probably going to get away with it. She wasn't sure how to tell Owen that her nightmare might never be over. Here he had agreed to help keep her safe until Nate was put away, and now, that might never happen.

He led her into his spare room, and she sat on the edge of the bed, preparing to tell him the whole ugly truth. "You know that I spoke to the cops yesterday, right?"

"I do," he said. Owen put her bag on the dresser and sat down next to her. "They questioned me while they were talking to you."

"Oh, I didn't know that," she admitted. "What did they ask you?"

"Just normal stuff—you know, how I know you and what I remembered at the bar," Owen said.

"What did you tell them?" she asked.

37

"I just answered their questions, why?" Owen asked.

"Well, I was wondering if you told the cops that you're my boyfriend like you told the nurses," she said. His cheeks tinted the cutest shade of pink and she couldn't help her giggle.

"You know about that?" he asked.

"I do," she admitted, "and I understand why you did it. They wouldn't have let you stay with me if you hadn't told them that. I actually appreciate you telling the nurses that you're my boyfriend. I don't think that I could have rested knowing that Nate could have gotten to me while I was in the hospital."

"Yeah, that's why I did it, but I have to admit—I kind of liked telling people that you are my girlfriend," he admitted.

"Really?" she squeaked. She was surprised to hear him admit something like that to her. Every time the nurses called him her boyfriend, she felt a bit giddy.

"Yeah, and I'm glad that you felt safe with me there. Now, you need to get some more rest," he said. Owen stood from her bed and pulled down the blankets. "Wait," she whispered. "I forgot to tell you what I needed to say."

"It will keep," he said.

"No, it won't," she insisted. "The officers that questioned me told me that they might not be able to lock up Nate because he had a solid alibi."

Owen nodded, "I'm sure that he does, but sooner or later, he'll slip up and they'll be able to put him away. Right now, you don't need to worry about Nate or where he is. You're here with me and I'll keep you safe, Tilly," he offered. Hearing him make her that promise made her heart melt just a little bit more.

"Thank you, Owen," she whispered.

"I'll have Maverick grab you some clothes and bring them over tonight. You okay with that?" She wasn't good with a

Riding Hard

stranger picking out her undergarments, but what choice did she have? "Don't worry—I'll just have him grab the basics and when you can safely look at a phone or computer screen again in about a week, you can do your own shopping and have everything delivered here." The problem was, that she didn't have a job to pay for any of the things she would need, and she hated taking handouts.

"We could just run by my apartment and grab my things," she offered.

"No," he breathed, "your place is probably being watched and we could lead danger right back here and then, we'd both be out of a home. You just have to be a little bit patient with me, Tilly. I'll make sure to get you home just as soon as I can." She worried that he would be true to his word and have to go home soon. She was just getting used to the idea of being at his place with him —alone.

"No rush," she said around a yawn. Tilly slipped between the sheets as he held them open for her and then, Owen tucked her in.

"I'll be back in an hour to wake you," he said, "sleep well, Tilly." He shut off the lights and walked out of the room, leaving the door open. "Just yell if you need me," he shouted back over his shoulder. Tilly settled into the cozy, warm bed and moaned at just how good it felt to be in a real bed and not a hospital bed. That thing was the most uncomfortable bed she had ever spent the night in, but Owen's spare bed certainly made up for one bad night's sleep.

Tilly closed her eyes and before she knew it, she drifted to sleep, letting the darkness consume her. Owen would be back in soon enough to wake her, and she planned on sleeping every available minute before he got back.

39

OWEN

It had been two weeks since he had brought Tilly home with him and he had to admit, he liked having her in his space. She was finally feeling better—stronger each day, and when he told her about Mace wanting to meet her, she insisted on joining him at the club tonight. He liked the idea of taking her with him because he wasn't going to go anywhere without her. He had made up an excuse last week when he skipped going to the club for church and he was prepared to do it again if it meant staying with her and keeping her safe.

"You're sure that it's okay for me to go with you to the bar?" she asked. "I haven't been there since the night of my accident." He hated that she called what Nate had done to her an "Accident". There was nothing accidental about what that asshole had done to her.

"It wasn't an accident," he grumbled.

"I know that but I'm not really sure what else to call it," she

Riding Hard

admitted. "I'm still just trying to come to terms with it all so cut me some slack." He loved how feisty she could be. Sometimes, he wasn't sure how he had kept his hands and all his other body parts to himself. It had been two full weeks since she had moved into his place and all he wanted to do was move her into his bedroom and make her his—not that she was ready for any of that from him.

"Sorry, and yeah, it's fine that you come with me to church," he said.

"Church?" she asked. The MC world was new to her, and he liked telling her about the world that he loved so much.

"Yeah—it's our weekly meeting at the club. Our Prez, Mace, likes to keep us all updated and church is a great way to do it. We're patching in two new guys, Gunner and Jagger, from our sister club. They seem like good guys, and we need members. We lost a few guys last year and the club just hasn't been the same."

"How did you lose them?" she asked. "Did they die in a gang fight with another club or something?" He couldn't help his laugh, even when she screwed up her face to show that she didn't like him laughing at her.

"Sorry, honey," he mumbled. "No, we don't have gang fights with other clubs. They left the club to go to another one or moved to another town or state. No deadly gang fights or anything that dramatic."

"Oh—good," she whispered. "I'd feel bad if you had to fight with other clubs and stuff like that," she said.

"So, you'd miss me if I died in a gang fight with another MC then?" he asked.

"Um, maybe a little bit," she said, pinching her thumb and finger together to give him a visual. "I might not have said it

41

since you brought me here, but I really appreciate you taking care of me out of the hospital and giving me a safe place to stay while I try to figure out what Nate is up to." She had thanked him just about every day that she was at his place, but he wasn't about to tell her that. She was still having issues with her memory and the doctor told him not to discourage her.

"That's good to know," he leaned into whisper. Every time he got too close to her, pushing Tilly from her comfort zone, she'd back away from him. But this time, she leaned into him. That was a good sign and one that he planned on exploring but now wasn't the time. He couldn't be late for this meeting since Tilly was the reason why they were having it. Mace wanted to patch in the new members and then talk about Tilly's attack at the bar. They were going to have to boost security around the place and Owen was all for helping with that. If he had to go into the bar for church, he would want to bring Tilly with him, and keeping her safe was his top priority. It's why he had beefed up security around his place since moving her in with him. Maverick had given him a hand with that task, and he had to admit, having his older brother around more was starting to become something that he could get used to. In some strange way, Tilly had brought them closer together when Owen was sure that the sexy red head might end up tearing them apart. As soon as Owen brought Tilly home with him, Mav backed off from pursuing her. If his brother found out that he still hadn't made Tilly his, he might give him some shit, but Mav seemed to know Owen's intentions toward his new ward.

"We need to get going," he said, backing away from Tilly. She was still leaning into his body, her eyes closed, and it was taking all his restraint not to kiss her. Did she want him to kiss her?

Riding Hard

That was something that he needed to figure out later too, but right now, they had to get to the bar.

"Let me just grab my jacket, and I'm ready," she said. She ran back to her bedroom and was by his side, ready to leave, in minutes. She looked damn near perfect in her jeans and sweater. She had done her makeup and hair, not that any of that mattered to him. Honestly, Owen liked her when she pulled her long red hair back into a slick ponytail and wore no makeup. But he had to admit, her bright red lipstick was really turning him on, and he worried that some of the guys at the club might feel the same way. There was no way that he'd ever let any of them get close enough to make a move on Tilly, but fighting off his buddies all night wasn't his idea of a good time.

"You look beautiful, Tilly," he almost whispered. He wasn't sure how she'd take his compliment, but the words were out of his mouth before he could even stop them.

"Really?" she squeaked looking her body up and down. "I still feel a bit groggy, so getting dressed up was a bit of a chore. I feel like I did the bare minimum." If this was her bare minimum, he wasn't sure that he'd be able to handle her best.

"Well, you look great. Listen, just stick by me tonight and you'll be fine." She snuggled into his side, and he was sure that he wasn't going to be able to keep his hands to himself much longer.

"Will do," she breathed.

They got to the bar about five minutes before church was supposed to start. He helped Tilly out of his pickup truck and tugged her against his side. "Remember, stay close to me," he ordered.

"Got it," she whispered back. She put her hand in his and he felt this insane sense of pride that he had no right to feel. They walked into the bar, hand in hand, and he felt all eyes on them as he settled down with her in the corner of the room. Most of the time, women weren't allowed in their clubhouse during church, but tonight's meeting had to do with his woman and Mace insisted that she attend. If the club's Pres insisted that someone attend church, they usually obliged.

Mace met them at the bar and held out his hand to Tilly. "I'm the Road Reaper's Prez," he said. "Mace."

"Good to meet you, Mace," she breathed, shaking his hand. "I'm Tilly."

"I've heard a lot about you and I'm sorry about what happened to you here at my club. I wasn't here that night, but I wish that I was. I would have killed that fucker for what he did to you." Owen knew how his Prez felt. He wanted just five minutes alone with her asshole ex-boss.

"I appreciate you saying that, but there was honestly nothing anyone could have done to stop Nate. He snuck in and out through the bathroom window. At least, that's what I've been told. My memory of that evening is still a bit sketchy, but the doctors all say that I might get them back at some point," she said. Owen hated that she still had gaps in her memory about that night, but maybe it was a good thing that she couldn't remember what had happened to her. Finding her laying on the bathroom floor was something that he wished he could forget too.

"Well, I just wish I would have been there that night," he repeated. Tilly nodded and smiled as Mace showed her to a

44

Riding Hard

corner booth in the back of the bar. "I hope you'll both join me tonight at my table," he said. Being asked to sit with the club's Prez was a big deal, even if Tilly didn't seem to pick up on that.

"We'd be honored," Owen quickly said, filling the silence. Tilly slipped into the booth and Owen slid in next to her.

"I'm going to get church started," Mace said. "I'll see you both later."

Owen waited for Mace to leave before leaning into Tilly. She still smelled like apples and cinnamon from when she sprayed her perfume earlier. A part of him wondered if she'd taste that way too. "Thanks for that," he whispered, trying to keep his cool.

"What did I do?" she asked.

"Well, you agreed to sit with Mace, and I appreciate that," Owen said.

"Oh," she said, waving him off, "that wasn't a big deal. He was kind to invite us to sit with him."

"It's kind of a big deal that he asked us to hang out with him," Owen said.

"You mean like when you get asked to sit with the cool kids at lunch in high school?" she teased.

"Yeah, you could compare it to that," Owen agreed.

"Isn't that your brother?" she asked, looking across the room at the front door.

"Yeah, that's Maverick. Will you be okay for a second while I run over to talk to him?" Owen asked. She smiled and nodded at him as he stood. He could feel her eyes on him as he made his way across the barroom, and he had to admit that he liked the way she watched him.

"I see you brought Tilly," Mav said, nodding over to where she sat.

45

"Yeah, Mace asked me to bring her along which worked for me because I wasn't going to leave her back at my place alone. Not with her fucking ex-boss still not showing his damn hand. That fucker got away with knocking her out, putting her in the hospital, and the cops aren't even going after him. They said that he was just a person of interest in the case, even though Tilly identified him as her attacker. He didn't even spend a night in jail."

"Yeah," Mav breathed, "I kind of ran by her sister's place to check on her and her kid this morning and my surveillance wasn't as stealthy as I hoped it would be. She caught be spying on her and her kid and well, I had to fess up that I was just checking in on them. She said she appreciated it, but then her husband showed up and I felt like an ass for even stopping by."

"You met her husband?" Owen asked. Tilly had told him a little bit about her sister, Melody, and how she worried that she was in over her head with her husband. Tilly wasn't sure if she was blowing things out of proportion or not, but she had a sick feeling that Melody's husband was abusing her. She made him promise not to tell anyone about her suspicions but hearing that the guy was an ass didn't bode well.

"Yeah, I met him. He really is an ass. He got in my face and told me that I didn't need to stop and check in on his family. I mean, I can't blame him for acting that way. If they were my family, I'd do the same. You know, some strange guy stopping by to check in on your wife and kid—that wouldn't play well for me either."

"I guess you're right. Has Melody had any news about Nate? Has he tried to reach out to her?" Owen asked. Tilly said that was her biggest fear—Nate going after her family. She seemed so selfless and that only made him want her more.

Riding Hard

"She said that she hasn't seen or heard from him, but I'm wondering if that was for her husband's benefit," Mav said.

"Do me a favor and let me tell Tilly that you stopped by her sister's place. I don't want to upset her while we're here," Owen said.

Maverick looked over at Tilly and smiled. "Um, she doesn't look too upset right now, bro. She looks pretty damn happy." Owen turned to find her surrounded by a half dozen bikers and groaned.

"What the actual fuck?" he asked.

"You left her alone and you know how the guys like to take advantage of a pretty woman left all by herself," Maverick reminded.

"They're fucking vultures," Owen grumbled. He crossed the bar room to the chorus of his brother's laughter, pushed a few of the guys out of the way, and pulled Tilly up from her seat. He could see the surprise register on her face before she gasped as he tugged her against his body.

"Back the fuck off," he barked, "she's mine." He sealed his lips over hers and when she wrapped her arms around his neck, he was sure that she as on board for whatever he planned to do next with her—but that would have to wait until he got her back to his place after the meeting.

Owen kissed her long and hard before he finally let Tilly up for air. He reluctantly let her go and stared down the assholes who hadn't taken the hint and were still hanging around Mace's booth. "Get the fuck lost," he shouted.

"Um, Owen," Mace said, "if you wouldn't mind finishing up your little show, I'd like to get on with church."

"Sorry, man," Owen grumbled. "I just had to set a few guys straight." He could feel Tilly's eyes on him still and he knew that

47

maybe setting her straight was also something he was going to have to do a bit more of. That worked for him because he had all night to go over things, just as soon as he got her home. And if he was able to convince her to move into his bedroom too—well then, even better.

TILLY

Tilly had spent two full weeks trying to figure out what to do about the sexy-as-sin biker who had taken her home from the hospital. He had nursed her back to health, put up with her crazy mood swings, and allowed her time and space to heal. Owen had kept her safe and helped her investigate just what her ex-boss might be up to. And still, she wasn't sure what to do about him.

Having Owen claim her in the middle of his club, telling all the other guys and even his older brother that she belonged to him—well, that just made her hot. The kiss was scorching and all she could think about was what he was going to do with her later when they were back at his place and all alone.

The rest of the night was a blur for her. She basically sat in the corner booth, pretending to listen to what was being said, and when Mace asked her to tell the guys what had happened to her in the ladies' room, she stared blankly back at the MC Prez.

"I'm sorry, what?" she squeaked.

"He wants you to tell the guys what happened the night you were attacked in the ladies' room," Owen said. The last thing she wanted was to have to talk in front of all the guys in the bar. She was still reeling from the kiss that Owen had laid on her.

"Um," she murmured. "There isn't much to tell. I went to the ladies' room and my ex-boss attacked me." Tilly wasn't sure what Mace was looking for here. Maybe he wanted more details and when he didn't speak after her short description, she began to ramble on, in detail, about why he took her purse and even described turning Owen down when he offered to buy her a beer. She looked over to find him watching her with Maverick and they were both wearing the strangest looks on their faces. Maverick looked amused. He even laughed out loud a few times during her rambling, but Owen looked a bit pissed and she knew that she was ruining everything.

"I'd like to leave now," she said. Tilly stood and moved out of the booth, heading for the back door that they had come in through just thirty minutes earlier. The bar was silent, and she wasn't sure if Owen was following her or not, but all she could think about was getting out of that place and into the cooler night air.

Tilly made it out of the bar and breathed in the cool air, letting it envelope her body. She took a deep breath and let it back out, trying to catch her breath. "Hey," Owen said, "what's going on?"

"What's going on is I didn't like having to talk in front of all those guys and I kind of freaked out," she whispered, sucking in another breath.

"Kind of freaked out is an understatement," he said. "You ran out of there like your ass was on fire."

"Well, I didn't mean to embarrass you, Owen, but I get

Riding Hard

nervous talking in front of a crowd—not that you would know that about me. You don't really know me at all."

He took a step toward her, and she backed up, running into the brick wall behind her. There was nowhere for her to go, and Owen seemed to take some secret delight in that.

"You didn't embarrass me, Tilly," he whispered. He put his hands on the brick wall behind her, essentially trapping her between the building and himself. "You make me crazy and turn me inside out. Hell, you turn me completely on. But you don't embarrass me."

"I do?" she squeaked.

"You do," he admitted. "I'm done pretending that I don't want you, honey. I want you more than I want my next breath. And as for knowing you, I was hoping that you'd give me the chance to get to know you, Tilly." He was saying everything that she wanted to hear from him, but it was as if her ears didn't want to believe him.

"You do?" she asked again.

"Yep," he whispered. His lips were so close to hers; that she could feel his warm breath on her face. He made her hot and all she wanted to do was wrap her arms around his neck and pull him into her body, but she knew that if she did, it would change things between them forever. Were they ready for that? No, the real question was if she was ready for that.

"Tilly," Owen breathed, "stop overthinking all of this and just do what you feel like doing," he said as if reading her mind.

"I'm scared, Owen," she admitted. The big biker crowded in closer, and she shivered.

"Are you cold?" he asked.

"No, I'm not cold," she whispered. "I'm worried that if we do this, things will change between us. I have nowhere else to go if I screw this up."

"You won't have to go anywhere, honey," he said. "I'll never ask you to leave. I like having you with me, and I wasn't kidding in there when I told the guys that you're mine. I want you to be mine more than anything, baby."

"Owen," she whispered. "I want that too," she admitted, wrapping her arms around his neck.

"Thank fuck," he whispered, sealing his mouth over hers. This kiss was different from the one he had given her in the bar. This one was more passionate, if that was even possible, and when his tongue slipped into her mouth to find hers, her damn knees nearly buckled.

"Woah," he breathed, pulling her into his arms. "You okay?"

"I'm good," she assured, "please don't stop, Owen." Tilly worried that if he took the time to think about what they were doing, he'd end up changing his mind about her and what he wanted from her. She knew that she was playing with fire, but she wanted Owen to scorch her.

He lifted her up his body and she wrapped her legs around his waist. "Here?" he asked.

"Yes," she agreed, "here."

"I wanted to take my time with you, Tilly," he whispered against her lips.

"You can take your time with me later," she insisted. "Right now, I just want you, Owen." She was giving him the green light that he had asked her for, and Tilly couldn't wait to see if he took her up on her offer or remained the gentleman who kept her at arm's length.

"This is going to be fast, honey. I don't want anyone to catch us out here." Hearing that someone could walk out and find

Riding Hard

them up against the building made it even more exciting for her. She always liked taking chances and doing things that might seem risky to others. Maybe that was what got her into the mess with her ex-boss and the hard drive that she stole off his desk.

"I'm good with that, Owen," she breathed. He pressed her back against the brick building and quickly undid the button and zipper to his jeans, making fast work of her jeans as he pulled them down her thighs. Owen ran the head of his cock through her wet folds, and she moaned at how good he felt. She whimpered for him to stop teasing her and he chuckled against her neck.

And when he took her, Owen covered her mouth with his own, taking in every little gasp and moan that she made. He filled her, making her cry out at how full she felt. "You feel so fucking good," he whispered to her.

"You do too," she breathed.

The noise from inside the bar was getting louder and she worried that the meeting was over. Owen looked back through the door and groaned. "We don't have much time, honey," he said. "I need you with me. Touch yourself," he ordered.

"What?" she asked.

"I want you to touch yourself. I want you to get off with me and we don't have much time. The meeting is over," Owen warned. She hesitantly snaked her hand down between where their bodies were joined and ran the tip of her finger over her clit. Owen pumped in and out of her body, pressing her against the hard brick and making no apologies for being so rough with her. Honestly, Tilly loved everything he was doing to her and when he told her to come with him, she couldn't help the way that her body responded to his demands. She shouted out his

53

name as she found her release, sure that everyone inside the bar would be able to hear her, but she just didn't care.

"You're fucking perfect," Owen praised as he found his own release, pumping his seed deep inside her body. He pulled free from her body and helped to quickly right her jeans. "Someone is coming," he warned.

"I thought you two left already," Maverick said, walking out from the back door.

"Um, we just stopped to talk," Owen lied. Maverick looked his brother over and smiled. Tilly was sure that he knew exactly what they were doing in the parking lot, but she hoped that he didn't question them.

"Right, well, you might want to do up your fly if you're just going to talk," Maverick teased.

"Oh, yeah," Owen said, pulling up his zipper. "Well, we better head home." He reached for her hand and Tilly didn't hesitate to take it. She was feeling a bit shy about being caught, and all she wanted to do was go back to Owen's place and crawl into bed—preferably his.

"Night you two," Maverick called after them. "Sweet dreams," Owen muttered something about his brother being an ass as he helped Tilly into his truck, causing her to laugh. Yeah, she was ready for bed and hoped like hell that what she and Owen just did in the parking lot wasn't the end of their night together.

They got home late and by the time she showered, Owen had moved her into his bedroom, insisting that she be in his bed with him. Tilly had no arguments about sleeping with Owen. In

Riding Hard

fact, she wasn't sure why she had put up such a fight to begin with. Being with Owen felt as easy as breathing now.

She was lying in his arms, almost asleep, when his phone chimed. He looked at the screen and sighed. "It's Maverick," he said. "He texted and wants to know if you are all right."

Tilly playfully wiggled her ass against his hand, and he chuckled. "Tell him that I'm more than fine now."

He grabbed his cellphone and shot Maverick off a text. "Done."

"That was nice of him to check on me," she said. "I didn't think that Maverick liked me very much."

"Um, he likes you. I guess he's just pissed that I ended up with the girl and he was left empty-handed," Owen admitted.

"Well, I like your brother," she said.

"Wait—you like Mav?" Owen asked. "What the hell, honey?"

"Why are you upset?" she asked. "You don't want me to like your brother?" She thought that he would be happy about his brother and his girlfriend getting along. Well, she liked to think of herself as his girlfriend now. Maybe he didn't think of her that way and that's why he seemed a bit put off by her declaration.

"No, I don't want you to fucking like my brother," he growled. "The only man I want you to like is me, Tilly."

"I do like you, Owen," she insisted. "I more than like you. I'm not seeing what the problem is."

"You said that you like Maverick and—" he started.

"And you think that I meant that I like him, like him," she finished. God, she was an idiot. She wrinkled up his nose and looked up at him. "He's not really my type," she admitted.

"Really?" he asked, "you're not just saying that?"

"No, I'm not just saying that," she admitted. "The only man

that I'm interested in is you, Owen." She wrapped her arms around him and snuggled in closer.

"Good to know, honey," he said.

"Although, it was kind of cute seeing you act all jealous," she teased.

"I was not jealous," he insisted. He wore an adorable scowl, and she couldn't help her giggle.

"Okay, well, it was still adorable," she insisted.

"Fine, but I can't help it if you find me irresistible," he said.

"I didn't say that I found you irresistible. I said that you were adorable," she reminded. "And if you keep gloating, I'll find that to be a lot less true."

"How about if I show you how adorable I can be?" he asked, rolling her body underneath his own.

"Oh, I like the way that you think," she praised. Tilly wrapped her arms and legs around him, loving the feel of his weight on top of her body.

"Prepare to be amazed," he teased.

Tilly giggled, "Bring it on, Owen," she whispered into his ear. Tilly wasn't sure how she had found the perfect man. Heck, he was actually the one who had found her, but letting down her defenses and giving into what she wanted with Owen was turning out to be the best decision she had ever made.

OWEN

Owen grabbed his cell phone from the kitchen counted and tried to silence it before it woke up Tilly. She was still asleep, just down the hallway, in his bed. He had kept her up during the night and he didn't want her to have to get up before she was ready.

"Hello," he whispered into his cell.

"Did I wake you?" a man asked.

"No," he breathed, "who the fuck is this?"

"Oh, yeah," the guy said. "Sorry, man. This is Jagger from the club." Jag was one of the new patch overs from a sister club. Owen wondered why Mace would have him call, but then again, maybe the guy was just trying to help out their Prez to show off a bit.

"What can I do for you, Jagger?" Owen asked.

"Nothing," Jagger said. "I just called to let you know that Mace is having an emergency meeting—club members only. No Ol'ladies."

"Okay, did he say what the meeting was about?" Owen asked.

"Nope, he just told me to call the guys and get everyone in here at about seven tonight. You good with that?" Jagger asked.

"Yeah, I'll make it work," Owen grumbled. He wasn't sure what he was going to do about Tilly since she wasn't feeling the best today. She had been dealing with an upset tummy for almost a week now and the last thing she'd want to do was get dressed and head out to his club for the evening.

"Great—only club members," Jag quickly reminded. Well, that would take care of him having to drag Tilly out with him but leaving her alone wasn't something that he wanted to do either.

"I don't know if I'll be able to make it then," Owen insisted.

"Don't you have someone who can sit with your woman while you take care of business here?" Jagger asked.

"No," Owen breathed. He wasn't about to tell this guy his life story or give him any information about his woman. "What's with all the questions?" Owen asked.

"Just trying to help out, man," Jagger insisted. "I just know that Mace wants you here, so make it happen." There was no way that he'd leave Tilly and bringing her along wasn't an option either.

"I'll see what I can do," he assured, ending the call. He tossed his phone back onto the counter and turned to find Tilly standing in the doorway, watching him.

"Trouble?" she asked. She was wearing his t-shirt and he wondered if she had on anything under it.

"No trouble," he lied.

"Then, why do you look like whoever was on the other end of that call said something that you didn't like?" she asked.

"Because he did, but that's not your problem. And it's no

trouble," he insisted. "I just need to decide what I'm going to do about it."

"How about you tell me what's going on and I can try to help you?" she asked. He hated to burden Tilly with any of his problems. She already had enough on her plate with the investigation that she was doing to look into what her boss was up to.

"You shouldn't have to worry about my issues," he insisted.

"But what if I like worrying about you and your issues?" she asked. Tilly wrapped her arms around his waist and he knew that there was no way that he'd be able to tell her no once she started touching him.

He sighed, "Fine," he agreed, tugging her into his body. "That was one of the new guys down at the club—Jagger."

"What did the new guy want?" she asked.

"The new guy wants me to leave you here and run down to the bar tonight for a special meeting that Mace has called," Owen admitted.

"Then you should go and find out what this meeting is all about," she said. "I take it that there is a no girls-allowed rule," she teased.

"Um, right," he said. "It's club members only tonight."

"Well then, you should go, and I'll be fine. You'll be gone what—an hour?" she asked.

"Probably, but that's not the point," Owen said. "I won't leave you here alone."

"I've been here alone before," she reminded. There were a few times that he had to run over to Mavericks for a few minutes and leave her at his place. He had the best security system he could build and knew that she'd be safe, but he still hated leaving her. Then, there were times when he had to run to a client's house or business to check on things. He had hired

59

another guy to help him with security system installations, but he still liked to meet with perspective clients face to face since it was his security firm that they were hiring. Every time he left Tilly, he felt guilty as hell and worried the whole time, but he would hurry back home to find her watching television or soaking in the bath, and he felt silly.

"I know that you have, but I just have a sick feeling about all this, in my gut. You know, like something bad is going to happen, but you don't want to admit it out loud."

"Don't be silly," she insisted. "Nothing bad is going to happen if you leave me alone for an hour to go to the club. Besides, it might be good for you to get out of here. You seem to be going a little bit stir-crazy lately." She was right—he was. He was worried about her ex-boss and why he hadn't shown his hand yet. The guy seemed to have gotten off scott-free in this mess and Tilly was still trapped at his place, putting her life on hold until she could figure out what was on that hard drive that she took.

"What will you do while I'm gone—you know, if I actually go?" he asked.

"I'll probably just sleep," she said. She had been sleeping a lot lately. Tilly had been dealing with a stomach virus that she just couldn't seem to shake. "I'm still not feeling one hundred percent," she admitted. "So really—you should go. I'm just going to get into bed and sleep until you come home."

He wasn't sure if it was a good idea to leave her still, but defying Mace might end up being a bad idea. His Prez wouldn't call a meeting if it wasn't important. And he wouldn't have had Jagger call him personally if he was okay with him skipping the meeting.

"Fine, I'll go, but you promise to call me if you need me?" he asked.

Riding Hard

"I promise," she agreed. "It's nice the way that you worry about me," she said.

"Well, it's something that you should get used to because it's not changing any time soon," he said.

"I think that I can get used to it," she agreed. "As long as you can get used to me feeling the same way about you, Owen." They hadn't really talked about feelings and all that stuff in the months that they had been together. Every time she brought up feelings, he changed the topic, avoiding feelings like the plague. Sooner or later, he'd find a way to tell her that he had fallen in love with her, but right now, he needed to get ready to run down to the club for church.

"We'll talk about that later," he promised.

"Mm-hmm," Tilly hummed as if able to see straight through him. She could too, and he wasn't sure if he liked that fact about her or not. "We'll talk later," she whispered, going up on tiptoes to kiss his cheek.

TILLY

Tilly thought that she had heard Owen pull into the garage, but when she rushed to the door to greet him, she realized that she had made one fatal mistake—unlocking the door for Nate. He was the one person she didn't expect, and she should have. Tilly let her guard down and that allowed Nate to push his way into Owen's house and shut the door behind himself.

"You're here," was all she could say as she backed from the kitchen into the family room.

"I am," he whispered. "Did you think that I'd never find you, Tilly?" She didn't think that he'd find her. In fact, she was trying to think of a way to convince Owen to lighten up on his security measures around her and let her go back to work. She missed being a part of the outside world after being cooped up for six months now. But there was one problem with wanting to get back to the real world—Nate was till going to be out there and

Riding Hard

now, having him standing in front of her, she suddenly realized that fact to be true.

"I was hoping that you wouldn't," she whispered. "I was hoping that you would figure out that I'm not a threat to you, Nate."

"Not a threat to me?" he questioned. "How can you say something like that to me after you went to the police and told them that I was the one who knocked you out at that bar?"

"You were the one who knocked me out, Nate. I know that six months have gone by, but you have to at least remember that far back, right?" she taunted. "And I'm the one with memory issues from when you gave me a concussion."

"I'd apologize for that, but I'm not sorry. You needed to learn a lesson, Tilly," he spat.

"Oh, and what lesson is that Nate? I should be careful who I work for because my boss could be a snake in the grass?" Yeah, maybe taunting him wasn't her finest decision, but she honestly didn't care.

"You needed to learn to keep your hands to yourself and not take things that don't belong to you," Nate insisted. "You took my hard drive, and I couldn't allow you to keep it. I have too many important things on there."

"Yeah, like what?" she asked. Tilly had no idea what was on that hard drive. She never even opened it. She just knew that whatever it was, it was enough for Nate to knock her out to take it back.

"Good try," he mumbled under his breath. "How about we get you settled and then we can have a little chat? Have a seat in that chair," Nate said. He wasn't waiting for her response, but she still felt the need to give one.

"I'm good with standing," she sassed.

63

He walked across the room and shoved her into the chair that sat behind her. "You'll sit," he shouted. Nate dropped the black duffel bag that he had on his shoulder. She hadn't noticed it before he tossed it to the floor with a thud.

"What's in there?" she asked. Nate didn't answer her as he pulled a handgun from the bag and laid it on the floor next to his leg. He then grabbed out some rope and started wrapping it around her ankles. Panic welled up inside of her gut as he tightly secured the ropes. If he tied her to the chair, she might never get out of this mess.

"Is that really necessary?" she asked. "I promise to behave."

He looked up at her and rolled his eyes. "Like you've ever behaved," he said. "I just need to make sure that you play nicely while I decide what to do next."

"You don't have a plan?" she taunted.

"Whether or not I have a plan isn't your concern," he insisted. "Now, shut the fuck up or I'll gag you." Tilly sat back in the chair and felt as though she was pouting, but what good would that do her? Nate didn't care if she was unhappy with this whole situation. He probably didn't care if she was ever happy again as long as he got what he wanted. The question was—what did he want from her? Tilly was sure that she wasn't going to like the answer to that question, so she refused to even ask it. Right now, she needed to concentrate on talking Nate out of whatever he was planning to do to her. Then, she'd find a way to get to Owen. All she needed to do was keep a cool head and stay one step ahead of her ex-boss.

Riding Hard

"Nate, you don't have to do this," Tilly whispered. "I've already told you that your secret is safe with me."

"Yeah, you'll forgive me if I don't believe you, Tilly," Nate grumbled. "I mean, you did steal my hard drive and begin this nightmare. I'm just finishing the mess you started." He tightened the ropes around her ankles and stood in front of her. Nate didn't look like the kind man who had hired her all those years ago. No, he looked deranged with his hair standing on end as though he had run his fingers through it worrying. He used to be her friend, but now, all she could see when she looked into his eyes was the lunatic that he had turned into.

"Please," she begged again.

"You know what—just save it," he shouted at her. She didn't want to wince or shy away from him as she did, but Tilly couldn't help but be afraid of him. She knew that he had an end game in mind, and it probably involved killing her. There was no way that he'd let her go again.

"You thought you could hide away over here, but you were wrong. You didn't believe that I wouldn't be able to find you over here at your new boyfriend's place, did you? I mean, sure, it took me some time to track you down, but hiding in town, in plain sight wasn't your best idea, Tilly. I thought that you were smarter than that, but I guess that the company that you've been keeping has really brought you down."

"Owen hasn't brought me down," she whispered more to herself. "You don't know him. You don't even know me anymore, Nate. It's been almost six months since I took that hard drive. You can't possibly think that you're still being investigated." Tilly knew for a fact that he was still being investigated but telling him that wouldn't help her case. The only way out of this mess was to hope that Owen came back early from his club's meeting, or she'd be able to talk herself out of it. She had always been a good talker—her mother used to tell her that it was her best attribute. In fact, her mom used to joke that if someone took her, she should just start talking and they'd turn around and bring her right back. It was a joke at the time, but now that she was in this situation, it was possibly the best advice she had ever gotten.

"You'll forgive me if I don't buy into the whole, 'They aren't looking into me anymore,' routine. You and I both know that corporate espionage doesn't just disappear." She knew part of what he was up to, but Owen and Mav weren't able to put all of the pieces together.

"I'm sure that it's not as bad as you think it is," she lied. It was probably worse, but she didn't want to make Nate fly off the handle and do something even more stupid than just kidnapping her. She needed time to figure out how to get out of this trouble and talking to him might buy her that time.

"You really have no idea just how bad this whole thing is, do you?" he spat. "I will lose everything if you have your way."

"This isn't my way," she countered. Fighting with him wasn't a good look, but she wasn't sure what else to do. "I never intended for you to lose everything, Nate. We're friends." Appealing to his sense of decency was probably a long shot, but she knew that her friend had to be in that madman, somewhere.

"But that's exactly what you did when you took my hard drive. Why couldn't you just keep your hands off my things, Tilly?" he asked.

"If it helps, I never even saw what was on that hard drive," she admitted. She hadn't either. She had taken it on a whim. She knew that Nate was up to something, and she was pretty sure that the hard drive would have some answers for her, but she had

Riding Hard

no idea that it would be enough to destroy his entire life. She would have probably taken it knowing that, but she might have thought things through a bit more. Heading straight to a biker bar to, "Think things through," wasn't the best plan. Plus, she never imagined that Nate would be tracking her car to find out where she went. But then, if none of this ever happened, she wouldn't have met Owen, fallen in love with him, and dreamed of a future that she wasn't sure he wanted with her. Did Owen want her long-term, or was she just his pet project, protecting her until this nightmare was over? That was a good question and one that she hoped to be able to ask him once she got free from the rope bindings that Nate had haphazardly tied around her ankles and wrists.

"You think that matters?" he asked. "It doesn't. You taking the drive was enough to send my partners into a panic. They plan on killing me if I don't take care of you, Tilly." She could feel herself swallow and was sure that she looked as nervous as she felt. Almost like a cartoon character worried about what was going to come next.

"Take care of me?" she gulped.

"You really have no clue, do you?" he asked. "Do you think that I'd go through all this trouble hunting you down, only to let you go once we talked things out? How dumb can you be, Tilly?" he questioned.

"Well, I was hoping that we'd be able to come to some type of compromise that might not include you having to murder me or anything like that," she breathed.

"Not only do my partners want me to kill you, but they also want that boyfriend of yours, and anyone else who might know about the hard drive, taken out too. You involved other people in this mess, so their blood is on your hands, not mine." That wasn't something that she could let happen. Owen and Mav were only trying to help her and getting them both killed wasn't something that she'd allow to happen.

"They had nothing to do with this. They don't even know about the hard drive," she lied. "Please, just leave them out of this."

Nate barked out his laugh and she knew that her pleas were falling on deaf ears. "You've always been a horrible liar, Tilly. Do you know the reason why I hired you?" he asked. She nodded and he sat down on the couch as if settling in for a story. "I hired you because you seemed completely inept to be able to do your job. It was something that my partners liked about you too."

"Your partners?" she squeaked. He kept talking about his partners and knowing that they were watching her too made her even more nervous.

"You don't really need to know about them, but they are the ones calling the shots," he insisted.

"Then why not let them take the fall for all of this?" she asked.

"Because I'm too deep into this nightmare," he shouted. "I hired you because you seemed to be able to keep your nose out of my business, but I was wrong. Instead, you turned out to be the thorn in my side who couldn't keep her sticky fingers off my stuff."

"What kind of trouble are you in, Nate?" she asked. The only thing he had divulged was that his trouble involved corporate espionage. Other than that, she had no clue as to what he was into with his mysterious partners.

"I'll tell you this much, you showing up at that biker club really messed things up. You have no idea just how much. As soon as they saw you walking into that place, they panicked. In

68

fact, they were the ones who got me into the bar to take back the hard drive. They wanted me to kill you there, but then changed their mind because it would draw attention to their place." Did he really mean to say that his partners were a part of Owen's club?

"Are you saying what I think you're saying, Nate?" she asked. "Your partners are a part of Owen's MC?" She had only met a handful of the guys and she just couldn't pin any of them as the "Bad guys" in this whole story. They all seemed to want to help her and Owen, but then again, she could be reading everyone all wrong. She had once believed that Nate was on the up and up, and that was a completely wrong assessment of her ex-boss.

"Now you're catching on," he sassed. "You really aren't that bright, are you, Tilly?" he asked. "I was wondering if you and that big oaf you're with would ever figure it out. Honestly, I was hoping that you would so that my partners might just take care of you themselves, but you always seemed to find a way out. But now, they're done waiting for you to figure it all out, so they came up with a plan to call your lover away and leave you all alone for me to take care of things."

"The meeting down at the club—it was a setup?" she asked.

"Ding, ding, ding," he shouted, "now she's getting it." She worried about Owen walking right into Nate's trap, but there would be no way that she'd be able to help him in her current situation.

"If you let me go, I can help you," she said. God, she even sounded desperate to her own ears. "We can go down to Owen's club and convince your partners that I don't know anything about what's going on. We'll tell them that I didn't even look at the hard drive."

"Sure, and they'll just believe you because you're so convincing," he drawled. "And then what? They'll just let you and your biker boyfriend walk?" he asked.

She tried to shrug through her bindings. "Yeah," she said.

"You are so naive," he taunted. "My partners won't let you or your boyfriend leave that bar once we show up there. Then, they'll come after me for fucking this all up. It's not going to happen, Tilly," he said. "I'm going to follow orders and finish this, once and for all." He stood from the couch and left the room, leaving her alone. Tilly quickly looked around and realized that there was no way out of this mess and when Nate got back from whatever he was doing in the kitchen, her time would be up. There was no way out and now, she knew it.

OWEN

Owen pulled into the parking lot at the bar and parked in the back. He looked over at Maverick and could tell that his older brother was thinking the same thing. "I have a bad feeling about all of this," he said. "Mace wouldn't call a meeting on a Tuesday night, out of the blue."

"I know, but I really didn't put much thought into his impromptu meeting until after you picked me up. We don't have to go in there," Mav said. He knew that, but if they didn't walk into the bar, they might not ever end this nightmare.

"No, I think that we need to figure out what's going on and the only way to do that might be going in there. I just need to know that you have my back," Owen said.

"Always," Maverick assured, "I'll always have your back, man." He pulled his gun from his shoulder holster and checked to see that it was loaded and ready. Owen reached across the dashboard and opened the glove compartment, pulling his own gun from it and checking the same.

They stepped out of the truck and walked to the back door of the bar to find Mace standing in the shadows. "You two want to tell me why you're here on a Tuesday?" he asked.

"Well, we thought that you called a meeting, but you standing there, asking us that, proves that this is a setup," Owen said.

"I didn't call a meeting," Mace agreed. "You want to tell me what's going on?" The one thing their Prez hated most was being kept in the dark. They should have called him when they got the call to come in, but Owen hadn't put it all together yet.

"Yeah, we both got a call about an hour ago to come in. Jagger said that you were calling an emergency meeting. I told you that this was a bad idea, man," Maverick said.

"You did not," Owen challenged. "Listen, we can argue about who was right and who was wrong later. Right now, we need to figure out what the fuck is going on. I need to get back to Tilly."

"You left her alone?" Mace asked.

"I did," Owen said. "I've done it before when we had church. I didn't think that it was a big deal."

"Shit, I'll send a couple of guys over there to check on her while we figure this all out," he offered.

"No," Owen almost shouted. "If we were called here tonight, then some of the guys might be in on this. We can't take the chance that we're sending in someone who might want to hurt Tilly. She's safe. I've got great security and she'd reach out if anything seemed out of place."

"All right let's go in and find out what this meeting is all about then," Mace ordered. "I some of my guys have double-

Riding Hard

crossed us, heads will roll." They followed their Prez into the back of the bar and found the place eerily quiet. The bar was usually crazy with guys drinking and carrying on, but tonight, there seemed to be none of that going on.

"Is anyone else even here?" Mav whispered.

"Not many guys showed up tonight," Mace admitted, "that's why I was surprised to see you two here." They walked into the bar and flicked on the lights. The place was dark, and they hadn't even seen the four guys sitting in the corner.

"Took you long enough," Jagger grumbled. "Gunner and I were beginning to take bets on whether or not you'd even show. I see you brought back up." He looked Maverick over as he tried to step in front of Owen.

"This is my fight," Owen insisted, trying to shove his brother out of the way, but he should have known better.

"I told you that I'd have your back and I meant it, man," Mav reminded.

"Same goes for me," Mace added. "What the fuck is going on guys?" he asked.

Jagger stood from the chair in the corner and walked across the room. "Well, you see, we've been planning this little meeting for a while now. We just had to make sure that none of the other guys got in the way. And well, Tuesdays are slow around here, so we picked tonight. We just never thought you both would show up or that you'd be here Mace. That part is unfortunate, but we'll just have to wing it."

"So, you've been working with Nate this whole time?" Owen asked, trying to put the pieces together.

"Actually, he works for us," Jagger bragged. "I guess we could be considered his silent partners, but we're calling the shots."

73

Gunner barked out his laugh, joining Jag in the middle of the empty barroom.

"Pun intended," Gunner said. Owen felt his blood run cold as he suddenly pieced the rest of the puzzle together. They had called him into the bar to get Tilly alone and he had a feeling that even with his state-of-the-art security system, she wasn't going to be as safe as he wanted.

"Who are they?" Mace asked, nodding to the two guys still sitting in the corner of the room.

They were the new guys in the club. Both Jag and Gunner had patched over from a sister club a few months ago. He should have known that they were bad news, but the two seemed to steer clear of the rest of the guys. The other two guys were new. Owen had never seen either of them before.

"They aren't important," Gunner insisted. "In fact, the only two people you need to be thinking about right now are those two," he said, nodding to both Owen and Maverick.

"I know those two," Mace growled.

"Yeah, but now, you need to decide if knowing those two is worth your life. You see, we can't let them walk out of here alive, and killing you wasn't part of the plan, but we will if we have to," he quickly added.

Mace's laugh was mean and Owen worried that if they all lost their tempers, none of them might make it out of this mess alive, and that wasn't an option for him since he wanted to get back home to make sure that Tilly was all right. "Let's just talk this through," he said. He knew that he and his brother were carrying, but then again, he was positive that the four guys staring them down right now were too. "We don't have to do anything rash."

"Ahh, the voice of reason," Jagger challenged. "But you see, your girlfriend went and got involved in something that she shouldn't have been. She went snooping around her boss's office and found a hard drive linking us to him and his company. We were using it as a front to launder money. Once she saw what was on that drive, all bets were off. We were just waiting for her to give herself up, and when we were finally able to locate her, we just needed to get you and big bro here to walk away and give us our chance to take her out."

"Who did you send?" Owen barked.

Jagger laughed again and it was taking all his willpower not to launch himself at him and take him down. That would do him no good because the other three guys were chomping at the bit to get their hands on him next. "Well, I guess I can tell you. I mean, it really doesn't matter now that you're here. You two won't be seeing each other again. I hope you were able to say a proper goodbye to your woman before you left home tonight," Jagger taunted. Now, Owen was just plan ready to fucking murder the guy.

"Who did you send?" he repeated.

"I sent over our not-so-silent partner, Nate. You see, he was supposed to come in here and take care of that bitch the night he attacked her and ran off like a pussy through the ladies' room window. He fucked things up royally that night and left us with a lot of messy loose ends. But we're going to fix all of that tonight. Nate's going to clean up his mistakes and we're going to take care of you two. I guess I just need to know where you stand in all this, Mace. You with them or us?" he asked.

"Them," Mace growled without hesitation. "I'd never back a fuck up like you, Jagger. I should have known that you were an ass from day one, but your other club vouched for you when you patched over. Was this always the plan? Did you join the Road

Reapers just to get to Owen and Mav?" Owen could hear the hurt in his Prez's voice when he asked his question and God, that made him feel bad. He already knew the guys' answer and it pissed him off that Jag and Gunner had used the Reapers just to get to him.

"They were here the night that Tilly came in here looking for a place to hide out," Maverick said. "I remember seeing them watching her and wondering if they were going to make a play for her too."

"Yeah, we weren't really interested in her. We had just followed her here after Nate let us know that she had stolen his hard drive. He had her car tagged and finding her wasn't really an issue. Plus, we fit right into places like this. Once we realized that Nate fucked up, we inquired about joining your little club. Our glowing recommendations were faked for our patch over and well, here we are."

"It was all a lie then," Mace said. He wasn't asking, more telling, and that felt like a kick in the gut to Owen.

"Yeah, sorry, Prez," Jag taunted. "I guess that we're just going to have to get on with it then. We were hoping to make it look like an accident. Maybe even blame a rival gang or something, you know. But with three of you now, that's going to be a little bit harder."

"Well, fuck, guys," Maverick said, "we can just leave, and you won't have to worry about any of that. Or," he said, pulling the gun from his holster, "we can just make your deaths look like an accident." He pointed his gun at Jag and Owen had to hand it to the guy, he didn't even flinch. Owen did the same, pointing his gun at Gunner.

"You are still outnumbered," Jag reminded. "Four guns to two," he said.

Riding Hard

"Three," Mace corrected.

"Four to three is still outnumbered," Gunner breathed.

"You know, for an asshole, your math isn't too bad," a man called from the front door as it swung open. Mav's twin brother Steel stood in the doorway holding a shotgun that had belonged to their father, wearing a shit-eating grin to match his brother's.

"You got my message," Maverick said.

"Yeah, you're just lucky that I was in town for a bit," Steel insisted.

"You were in town and didn't bother to let us know?" Mav asked.

"Um, can you two bicker like old women later?" Owen asked. "It's good to see you, brother, but my girl is being held by her asshole ex-boss and I'd like to get back home to kill the fucker before he hurts her."

"Right, you go get your woman and we'll handle these assholes," Maverick said. He walked across the bar room and held his gun at the two guys in the corner. "They'll cooperate if they know what's good for them. I mean, my twin brother over there is lethal in about a dozen different countries."

Steel shrugged, "Probably more than a dozen, but who's counting? It's good to see you too, little brother. You do what you have to do and report back to us when you are both safe. I can't wait to meet your girl."

"Will do," he said, looking back over his shoulder. "Thanks for everything you guys," he said. "I don't know what I would have done without you three." Mace, Maverick, and Steel grumbled something collectively about him being a mushy pussy, making him laugh as he made his way back out of the bar. He ran to his pickup and said a little prayer that he'd be able to get to Tilly before it was too late. He was going to introduce her to

77

his oldest brother, Steel, and then, he was going to convince her to become his bride. It was time he let her make an honest man out of him and there was no way that he'd be letting her go just because her crazy ex-boss was out of her life. He was in love with Tilly, and it was about time that he told her.

TILLY

Tilly felt as though she was holding her breath waiting for Nate to come back to the family room from the kitchen. She knew that as soon as he did, her time would be up. That thought scared the hell out of her, but not knowing what he planned to do next, or even where he was, was even more terrifying.

"Come on and answer your fucking phone, Jag," he shouted from the other room. She was sure that he was talking about the new guy down at the club, Jagger. He and another guy named Gunner had joined the Reapers about the same time that she had hooked up with Owen. In fact, every time Owen took her into his club for a meeting, she noticed the two of them there. They were always watching her too, but she never really put two and two together and came up with them being her ex-boss's silent partners.

"Fuck," Nate shouted, and Tilly knew that her time was just about up. She closed her eyes as she heard him walking out of the kitchen and back to her. Tilly was sure that as soon as she opened her eyes, her life would end. Instead, she heard a loud thud and opened her eyes to find Nate lying on the floor in front of her with Owen standing over him.

"Owen," she sobbed.

"Hey, honey," he breathed. "I'm sorry that I left you alone and that this asshole got to you."

"You didn't know," she cried. "He has partners, and they are part of your club. I think it might be Jagger and Gunner—the new guys." Owen kneeled in front of her and nodded as he freed her ankles from the rope bindings.

"I know," he said. "They were waiting for Mav and me when we got to the bar. Luckily, Mace was there too and my brother, Steel showed up."

"Maverick's twin?" she asked.

"Yep," Owen breathed, "apparently, Mav called him and filled him in on what was happening he showed up just in time and well, as soon as everything was under control at the bar, I took off for home. I shouldn't have left you. This whole thing was a setup and I fell for it like an idiot."

"You couldn't have known. We had no idea that Nate had partners. He told me that he was working for them and that they wanted me dead. I guess you got here just in time to stop him from following through with their orders. I just can't figure out what they were doing though. Why would he need partners?"

"Jagger and Gunner were using his company to launder money. They weren't really his partners, more like his bosses. They were moving their dirty money through the corporation and giving Nate a cut. And the greedy bastard was fine with it all. He made the hard drive as backup, in case things went sideways. When you took the drive from his desk, he

Riding Hard

had to come clean with Jag and Gunner and that's when they found you at the bar. They were there the night we met."

"They were?" she squeaked. She didn't remember much about that night, especially after Nate had knocked her out. Her head injury really messed with her memories of that night.

"Yep, and Nate wasn't supposed to just knock you out. He was supposed to kill you. But thankfully, he's a giant pussy and couldn't follow through. You were a loose end and Jagger and Gunner wanted to get rid of you."

"That's what Nate said," she breathed. "I was so scared that he'd actually go through with it this time." She looked Nate over and back up at Owen. "Did you kill him?" she asked.

"Naw," Owen said. "I just knocked his ass out. The cops are on their way. I called them on my way over here."

"What about Jagger and Gunner?" she asked.

His smile was mean, and she suddenly wished she hadn't asked. "The guys are taking care of them. But I told the cops to go to the bar too, just to keep Maverick from killing them. My brother has anger issues."

"I picked up on that," she teased. "Is this nightmare really over?" she asked. He finished freeing her and pulled her into his arms. Tilly felt safe for the first time since he left her.

"It is," he agreed. "And this time, Nate here will go away for a long time. He won't get out of it again. We have the proof that we need to put him, Jagger, and Gunner, away for the rest of their lives, now that we can add kidnapping and attempted murder to the list of charges that they are facing."

"Good," she breathed. Tilly had so many questions that she wanted to ask next, but she wasn't sure where to begin. The biggest question she had was what happened between the two of them next. She had been living with Owen for so long now, she wasn't sure that she even had an apartment to go home to.

"I guess it's safe for me to go home then," she whispered.

"Tilly, I need to tell you something," he said. She held her breath and nodded, preparing herself for the worst. "I had to let your apartment go a few months ago. You weren't paying rent and well, I asked your landlord to pack up your stuff and put it into storage for you."

"You did?" she asked. "Why didn't you tell me?"

"Because I didn't want you to feel trapped. I wanted you to think that you had choices and that you'd actually chose to be with me." She would have always chosen him, not that she had told him that yet.

"Owen, I want to be with you," she said. "I would have chosen you."

"You would have?" he asked.

"Of course. You could have told me about my apartment," she insisted. "I would have understood."

"There's so much that I haven't told you, Tilly," he breathed.

"There's more?" she asked.

"Yeah," he whispered.

"Like what?" she asked.

"Like the fact that I'm in love with you and want you to be my wife," he blurted out. Tilly couldn't help the warm tears that spilled down her face as she quickly nodded her agreement. "Is that a yes?" he asked.

"It's a yes," she agreed. "But are you sure?"

"When I realized that tonight's meeting was a setup, I couldn't think about anything that I wanted more. I wanted to get home to you to make sure that you were safe and when I found that asshole here, I wanted to kill him, I really did. But I knew that if I went to prison, I couldn't marry the woman of my dreams."

"That's me, right?" she sobbed.

"That's you," he agreed. "I want to spend my life with you, Tilly."

"Well, that works for me," she agreed, "because I'd like to spend the rest of my life with you, Owen." He picked her up and spun around with her as the cops came in through the back door that he had left open.

"We're back here," he shouted. "The guy who broke in is out cold." He pointed to Nate who was still lying on the floor, never letting go of Tilly. That worked for her because she wasn't ever going to be letting Owen go again either. She had finally found her Prince Charming disguised as a sexy-as-sin biker and for the first time in her life, she felt like the lucky one. Stealing that hard drive was the best mistake she had ever made, followed closely by deciding to hide away in a biker bar. All her past mistakes led her to Owen, and that made her the luckiest woman on the planet.

TILLY
PROLOGUE

Tilly wasn't sure how she was going to tell Owen that she was pregnant, but her time was running out. She was starting to show and there were only so many ways to hide her little bump from the man who saw her naked every day. Tonight was the night—she was going to finally tell him. Just as soon as he got home from meeting with Maverick about becoming his business partner in the security firm that he was building. Maverick had expressed interest in working with Owen part-time, but he was hoping to convince him to come in as a full partner.

He walked in through the back door and tossed his truck keys on the counter, just as he had most nights. "You're home early," she said.

"Yeah well, that's because my brother is an asshole," Owen grumbled. "The big oaf will only commit to part-time working with me, even with buying in as a full partner. He said that he doesn't want to give up his bike shop, even though I know that he doesn't really love what he does anymore. He started that shop after our mother died. It put a roof over our heads and food in our bellies, but he loves security work, he's just too stubborn to admit it."

"I'm sorry," Tilly said, rethinking her plan to tell him about the baby. They had only been married for a month now, and she didn't realize she was pregnant, but she was about three months along. Her doctor told her that the signs were all there, but she was just ignoring them. She was nauseous and had missed periods, but with everything going on with her ex-boss, Nate, she didn't pick up on all the signs.

She didn't realize that she was crying until Owen wiped away a tear from her cheek. "You want to tell me what's going on or should I tell you?" he asked.

"What?" she questioned.

"I've been waiting for you to tell me for months now, Tilly," he whispered. "You're pregnant, aren't you?" he asked.

"No," she sobbed. "Yes," she said, letting him pull her into his body. "I just found out. How did you know?"

"I started to figure it out when you were sick for so long. I thought it was weird that you were sick in the mornings and then fine by lunchtime. You were tired too," he reminded.

"Well, if you were picking up on all the signs, why didn't you fill me in?" she asked.

"I wanted to let you figure it out in your own time. I figured that if you knew, you'd tell me when you were ready, and if you didn't know, sooner or later, you'd find out. I just didn't want to rush you," Owen insisted.

"That's why I love you," she whispered. "You really are the sweetest man."

Riding Hard

"Hey, don't go spreading that around," he grumbled, making her laugh. "I have a reputation to uphold."

"Of course you do," she agreed. "Seriously though, are you okay with all of this? We've only been married for a month now."

"None of that matters to me," he said. "I'm thrilled about there being a baby. The question is, are you?" he asked.

"I haven't had much time to digest all this, but I think that I am," she sniffled. "I saw my doctor a few days ago and have just been waiting for the right time to tell you. I guess you were just waiting for the right time to tell me," she said. "We make quite a pair."

"We sure do," he agreed. Tilly wrapped her arms around her biker and knew that with Owen by her side, she'd never have to worry about telling him anything.

"I was afraid to tell you," she admitted.

"Hell, honey," he breathed, "I was afraid that I'd be the one to have to tell you, but it all worked out. It usually does."

"How did I get so lucky?" she asked.

"You stole a hard drive from your boss and stumbled into my club's bar," he reminded.

"Well, I guess being a thief really paid off for me," she teased.

"Me too," he said, tugging her close. "Me too."

The End

I hope you enjoyed Owen and Tilly's story. The next two books in the trilogy are available now on Amazon! Don't miss book two of the Dirty Riders MC Series, coming in January 2024. Here's a sneak peek at Riding Shotgun!

MELODY

Melody Newton didn't really know her self-worth. She was never taught to stand up for herself and she had the bruises to prove it. But now, she was going to get a crash course in what it meant to stand her ground and give a damn about herself. Now, she was going to finally tell her good-for-nothing husband to hit the road. She had caught him sneaking around on her again, and this time, she had no forgiveness left to give him.

Adam walked into the kitchen and kissed her cheek, just as he always did before dinner. That was when she'd make a fuss about asking him how his day was and tell him about what she and their two-year-old daughter, June, did together while he was supposedly at work. But that wasn't going to happen tonight because she knew where he had been all day. Adam had spent all afternoon at the sleazy motel on the outskirts of town with some whore he probably had picked up a disease from. Melody knew this bit of information because her loving husband had used his credit card to pay for both as if he just didn't give a fuck about her finding out what he was doing—or in this case, who.

"How was your day?" he asked.

"My day?" she questioned. "Well, my day was very exciting. You see, I took June to the grocery store to pick up some groceries," she started.

"Yeah, I was going to ask what was happening with dinner. You haven't even started it yet? And where is our daughter?" June was usually sitting in her highchair, anxiously waiting for dinner, but Melody had gotten her sister, Tilly, to babysit June for the evening, so that she could face down her soon-to-be ex-husband. That's how Melody was getting through any of this right now. She just kept thinking that Adam would be her ex-husband, and she'd be able to start her life all over again. This time, she'd go it alone because there was no way that she'd allow another man to lay one finger on her ever again.

"Tilly took June for me," she said. "And dinner isn't ready, and it's not going to be ready, because my credit card was declined at the store. We're over our limit."

"Well, shit," he grumbled, pulling a beer from the fridge and popping off the top. "I'll put some money in the bank in the morning." She watched as Adam took a long swig of his beer and slammed the bottle down to the kitchen table, causing her to jump. "Since your sister has June, what do you say you and I have a little bit of fun, and then I'll take you out for a burger." The thought of Adam laying one finger on her repulsed her. He still smelled like the cheap hooker that he had spent the whole afternoon fucking.

"No thank you," she breathed.

"What do you mean by, 'No thank you?'" he asked.

"I mean that I don't want to have any fun with you, ever

Riding Hard

again, Adam. It means that I know why my credit card was over the limit and I couldn't buy food for our daughter. You used my card to pay for a whore and a motel room, didn't you?" she spat.

"You watch your fucking mouth, Melody. I told you that I wasn't going to do that again, and I haven't," he said, keeping up with his lie. If given the chance, Adam would rather die than claim the truth. But she knew the truth, even if he wouldn't say it out loud. He had cheated on her before, with her best friend from high school. Yeah, that one hurt like a bitch, but she forgave him. Melody was six months pregnant and a fool for thinking that staying with Adam was better for her and her unborn child than leaving him. She should have gotten out then, but she was too afraid to make a move that would cost her the roof over her head, so she stayed, and things went from bad to worse.

After he swore that he'd give up cheating on her, he got angry. It was as if he blamed her for not allowing him to screw around. Adam started getting rough with her and after a few times pushing her around and shouting at her, he finally hit her. She took it too, not wanting to cause waves. A part of her believed that she was responsible for his anger. She could deal with his anger, it was his cheating that broke her heart, so she stayed.

But now, finding out that he had cheated again, she felt numb. Melody was ready to walk out. Her and June's bags were packed and in the trunk of her car. Tilly said that they could stay with her and her new husband, Owen, for a while until she could get back on her feet. She had a plan and for the first time in her life, Melody felt like she had some self-worth.

She defiantly raised her chin to Adam as if daring him to hit her. "You did cheat on me, Adam," she insisted. "I have the credit card records to prove it. You've been going to that motel again, and this time, you've been paying for whores. Did you really believe that I wouldn't find the charges?" she asked.

"Maybe I just didn't fucking care if you found them," he spat. Adam sucked down the rest of his beer and grabbed another one from the fridge. If he continued drinking at this pace, she only had a small window of opportunity to let him know that they were done.

"I want a divorce," she said, "cutting right to the chase."

"Well, that's just too fucking bad," he shouted. "You and I are married, for better or worse, and you're not leaving me."

"I am leaving you and I'm taking June with me. I want a divorce and I'm going to go to a lawyer tomorrow. I'm sure that my credit card records will be enough to prove that you've been cheating on me." He put the new bottle of beer on the table and stepped closer to her. He smelled like cheap perfume and pussy. God, it made her want to gag, but she held it back. There was no way that she'd show any weakness around him ever again. She had already done enough of that to last a lifetime.

She stared him down and when he smiled and turned away, she thought that he was going to pick up his beer and leave her alone, but she was wrong. Adam quickly turned back and punched her so hard in the face that she landed on her ass, and damn if she didn't see stars.

"You feel better?" she slurred. She was sure that her eye would swell shut in a matter of minutes and he was only getting started—that she knew from experience.

"Not yet, but I plan on hitting you until I do," he growled.

"That's usually your plan, asshole," she said, sitting up from the kitchen floor. He stood over her and she smiled up at him, knowing something that he didn't gave her a second wind.

Riding Hard

"Why the fuck are you smiling at me, bitch?" he spat.

"Because for the first time, in a damn long time, I think I'm actually going to win this one," she said.

"You think that you can beat me?" he asked. Adam clenched his fist, an act that usually made her cringe, but this time she didn't feel anything. She had an ace up her sleeve—a large biker who stood in the doorway to her kitchen, and damn if he didn't look pissed off enough to tear Adam limb from limb.

"She might not be able to beat you, but I'm pretty sure that I can," Maverick growled. God, he was her knight coming to save her and she'd take it, even if she had just mentally sworn off all men forever.

"Who the fuck are you?" Adam shouted, turning his back on her. That's how he treated her—always underestimating Melody and thinking that she'd never retaliate. She was ready to take her stand, and when she found her feet, grabbing the frying pan from the stove top, she swung it at the back of Adam's head, knocking him out. He fell to the kitchen floor with a thud, and she tossed the frying pan to the ground.

"Hey, Maverick," she breathed, "can you call the police for me? I need to make sure that I didn't just kill my soon-to-be ex-husband."

He shook his head at her and smiled. "I knew that I liked you, kid," he said, calling her by that annoying little nickname he used for her. Melody knelt down to find that Adam still had a pulse. She stood, not sure if that was a good or bad thing. One thing was for sure, he wouldn't let her retaliation go unpunished and there was no way that he'd underestimate her again.

MAVERICK

Maverick Blaine knew something was up when he showed up at his brother's house and found him and his new bride babysitting Melody's kid. As soon as he walked into their house, the toddler made a beeline for him and begged to be picked up. He didn't mind kids, really, and Melody's brat was the cutest one he knew. He asked her where her mama was, and she just smiled back at him, giving him that blank stare that she usually gave him as she checked him out. June was fascinated by his beard and tats. He just wished her mom felt the same way about him, but Melody was a married woman, and he wouldn't cross that line, no matter how badly he wanted to.

Mav asked Tilly where Melody was, and she told him that her sister had some things to work out with her husband. That was all he got from her before she took June from him and whisked her off to the bathroom for a bath. It wasn't until he found his brother sitting in the kitchen, drinking a beer, that he got a

Riding Hard

straight answer about what was going on. That was when Owen told him that Melody had caught her scumbag husband cheating on her, again. He couldn't believe that anyone would cheat on her once, let alone twice. Hell, the woman he knew was sassy and confident and would never let some loser cheat on her.

Owen went on to tell him that he thought that letting Melody go back to her house to face her husband alone was a bad idea. He said that the asshole liked to smack Melody around and that's when Maverick lost it. He questioned his brother for letting Melody face that jerk alone and then stormed out of the house, mumbling something about needing to beat his little brother's ass.

He was right to show up at Melody's house unannounced too. When he got there, he snuck into the back kitchen door and found her husband standing over her, shouting that he was going to beat the shit out of her. And from the looks of Melody, who was already lying on the floor, he had already started. It took all his restraint not to run in and pummel the guy. And when Melody stood and hit the fucker in the back of the head with a frying pan, he felt a sense of pride that he had no right to feel about her. She was one tough chick and had had the physical and mental scars to prove it.

He called the police, and they showed up at her house, taking Melody's statement and arresting her husband for abuse. Maverick corroborated her statement, telling the cops that she acted in self-defense, and how he had found her on the floor after her husband had hit her. Mav's only regret was that Melody didn't kill the fucker. He was going to be taken to the hospital, to get checked out, and then, they were going to hold him until his bail hearing. He'd get out and then, he'd probably go after Melody and her kid, and Mav wouldn't let that happen. He just had to figure out how to convince her to let him take both her and June back to his place. Her ex would look for her at home first, and then, when he couldn't find her there, he'd head over to Tilly and Owen's place. His brother could handle the guy, but Mav didn't want Melody or June to have to go through any of that shit. Her asshole ex didn't know where he lived and that would give them both a safe haven while Melody figured out her next move.

He watched as the last of the cops left and Melody looked around her kitchen. "What now?" she asked.

"Now, we get you out of here," he said.

"Oh, yeah," she breathed. "I forgot all about calling my sister. She must be worried to death about me."

"I called Owen and filled him in. June is asleep and safe," he said, knowing that would be her next question. The few times that he was around Melody and her kid, he could tell that she was a great mother. He just had no idea that she was dealing with an abusive asshole at home.

"Thank you for doing that," she said. "God, what am I going to tell June about her father?" she asked. He really didn't have any answers for her. His own father was an asshole, and his poor mother was constantly covering for him and his bad behavior. But he and his brothers knew the deal. His father was a jerk and when he happened to be around, things were awful. Mav knew how much his mother struggled when his father would take off. She worked two jobs putting a roof over his, Steel, and Owen's heads and food on the table. The thing was, he and Owen were so much happier when their old man was gone, and he had a feeling that June would feel the same way about her father not sticking around.

"When she's old enough, you'll tell her the truth. Tell her

Riding Hard

how her brave mother stood up to a man who liked to beat her up. Tell her how strong her mom is, but I'm sure she'll already know all about it."

"Thank you for saying that, Mav," she whispered, swiping at the tears that were running down her cheeks. "I'm sorry I'm crying. I guess it's just been a long day. I need to get over to Tilly's. She's expecting me."

He grabbed her hand and she flinched, making him feel like a complete ass. Of course, she'd react to him that way. She had just had the shit beat out of her—Melody had the black eye to prove it. "I'm sorry," he said. "I'd never hurt you, Melody."

"I—I know that, Maverick. I'm just a little shaky is all. I didn't mean to react that way."

"I just wanted to talk to you about staying with Tilly and Owen," he said.

"Okay," she breathed, "is there a problem with me staying with them?"

"Not a problem," he said, "more like an issue. Owen is worried that after Adam gets out of jail, he'll come looking for you here."

"Right, and when he can't find me here, he'll search for me at Tilly and Owen's place. God, I'm an idiot. He doesn't want me there because he's worried that I'll put them in danger."

"No," Maverick said, "God, I'm screwing this all up. He's worried that he won't be able to protect you, Tilly, and June all by himself."

"Yeah, that makes sense," she said. "Um, I guess I'll just have to find another place for me and June to stay—you know until everything dies down with Adam." He didn't want to be the one to tell her that things might never die down with her soon-to-be ex. If he got out of jail, he might not ever leave her and June alone.

"How about you stay with me?" Maverick asked. She looked up at him as if he lost his mind, and maybe he had.

"That's not a good idea," she said. "I mean, won't I be putting you in danger then?"

He couldn't help laughing at the idea of him being put into danger by a mom and her kid staying with him. "I think that I'll be able to handle him if he shows up to my door."

"Yeah, you do seem capable," she said, looking him over. He liked the way that she took in every inch of him, letting her eyes roam his body. They had always had some unspoken connection, but he never acted on it knowing that she had a husband waiting for her at home. "But I don't want to put you out," she insisted.

"You wouldn't be putting me out at all," he assured. "I can keep you and June safe, I promise, Melody." He was making promises and getting involved—two things that he swore that he'd never do. But then again, Melody had him doing things he never thought he'd ever do, and with her, playing the protector, felt right.

Riding Shotgun (Dirty Riders MC Series Book 2) universal link-> https://books2read.com/u/bOeMzQ

And as a special bonus, here's a look at Riding Steel (Book 3 of the Dirty Rider Series)! It's available now for preorder here-> https://books2read.com/u/mdqy9w

STEEL

Steel Blaine watched as Justice paced in front of his makeshift desk. He really needed to go shopping for office furniture, but who had the time? Since joining his two brothers in their security team, he didn't have one second to himself. His folding table worked just fine as a desk, and it also allowed him to believe that he'd be able to pick up and move on if necessary. A big, heavy desk would void that possibility and that wasn't something he was willing to think about right now. No, right now, he had to decide what to do about the sexy blond nervously pacing in front of him.

"I know it sounds crazy, Steel, but I can feel him out there watching me. I've already been to two cities for my book tour, and he showed up at both of them," Justice said.

"Wait, you've seen this guy?" Steel asked.

"I have and he's not shy about letting me know that he's around." Justice pulled her phone out of her purse and handed it over to him. "Those are all texts from him." He read through the disgusting texts and grimaced at the ones that were explicit requests that made him want to take the job for her on the spot.

"He has your number?" Steel asked, already knowing the answer to his question. He was holding the proof that the guy had her phone number.

"Yeah. I'm not sure how he got it, but he's been texting me for months now," she admitted.

"Jesus, Justice," he growled. "Why didn't you come to me sooner, or at least change your fucking number?" he asked.

"Because we didn't leave things on the best terms," she reminded. Justice was right. The last time he saw her, he acted like an asshole. The last thing she probably wanted to do was reach out to him and ask him for his help.

"Plus, I've been kind of busy with my writing, and I guess that I was just hoping that this mess would go away on its own," she admitted. He knew just how busy she had been with her writing. Justice had built quite a name for herself over the past year, even landing a seven-book series deal with a big publisher. He had followed every step of her impressive career, but there was no way that he'd admit that to her. She already had one stalker; he didn't want her to think that he was stalking her too.

"Obviously, this guy isn't going to go away if he's still sending you these messages and following you around on your book tour," Steel said.

Justice rolled her eyes at him, "Obviously," she grumbled. "Listen, maybe coming to you for help was a mistake. I should have realized that you'd still be pissed off at me. I just never imagined that you'd be holding a grudge or anything as childish as all that." She took her phone back from him and put it into her purse. "Tell Owen and Mav that I said, 'Hey'," she said, turning to leave.

Riding Hard

"Justice, wait," he growled. The words were out of his mouth before he could even think them over. She was right—he was acting like a child and that wasn't how he wanted things to play out between him and Justice. "I was an idiot back in high school," he admitted. He was too. Justice was the prettiest girl in the whole school, and she liked him. His problem was, that she told him that she liked him, and his stupid mouth got in the way of him giving her the words back. In fact, Steel had made up some stupid lie about not liking her and liking her best friend, Julie, instead. He took things too far by asking Julie out to prom and that was about the time that Justice had quit talking to him. He graduated, watched his mom die from cancer, joined the Navy, and he didn't look back. Steel stayed away from home for as long as possible, letting his twin brother, Maverick, and his little brother, Owen, handle everything on the home front. He wasn't the kind of guy looking to put down roots and Justice was the kind of girl who would have required that commitment from him.

"Wait for what, Steel?" she asked. "Wait for you to break my heart again? Wait for you to take off again when things get too hard to handle. What am I waiting for now?" she asked. He deserved that from her. She had every right to question him and the reasons why he was asking her to wait.

"I'm sorry about all of that, Justice," he insisted. "I should have never asked Julie out. I lied about even liking her and took things too far." He had admitted all of that to Julie at prom, ruining their whole night together, but he just couldn't help himself. Self-sabotage was his go-to move, and he was pretty damn good at it.

"Yeah, Julie told me all about what you said to her and how you hurt her. How could you do that to her at prom?" she asked.

"Because I'm an ass," he said. "But you already knew that. I'm sorry for all of it," he said. "I should have been honest with you from the beginning, but I wasn't."

"Yeah, and what would that have looked like, Steel?" she asked. "You know—you being honest with me."

"It would have looked like me telling you that I liked you too, but I was too afraid to say those words out loud. My mom was sick, and we didn't know how sick until Mav and I graduated. Watching her fade away was a lot for teenage boys to handle. I guess I was afraid that if it told you how I felt about you, you'd disappear too, just like she did. It's why I've been away from home for so long now." The only reason he had come home was to be closer to his brothers. It didn't hurt that Justice was still in town and still single, but he wasn't holding out hope that she'd ever forgive him for how he treated her back in high school.

"I'm sorry that you had to go through all of that, Steel. I wish you would have let me in to help you, but that's not what I need right now," she said. "I'm not standing here telling you that I like you," she said. "I'm asking you to let me hire you. I need someone to go with me on the rest of my book tours this year, and I was hoping that you'd want the job. I don't trust a lot of people, but I trust you, for what it's worth." Hearing her say that was worth more than she'd ever know. There was no way that he'd let her down again.

"I'll take the job," he quickly agreed.

"Wait—what?" she asked.

"I'll take the job," he repeated.

"You will?" she asked again.

"Yep," he said.

"It's going to be a lot of travel," she said.

Riding Hard

"I'm okay with travel, as long as you're good with paying my travel expenses," he teased.

"Um, yes," she said. "I will pay for everything. Thank you, Steel," she said. Justice held out her hand to him and he walked around his makeshift desk to shake it.

"You are welcome," he said.

"Oh—just one other thing," she quickly added. "I don't want anyone knowing about my stalker—especially not my publisher."

"Okay, can I ask why?" he asked.

"Because the guy who's stalking me used to work for my publisher and I don't want to lose my contract with them. Can you make me that one promise?" she asked. "They can never know." Well, that solved the mystery of how he got her number and how he seemed to know where she was going to be and when. All Steel had to do now was figure out why this asshole was going after Justice and then, he'd be able to keep her safe.

"Deal," he agreed. "No one will know about your stalker."

"Or that you're my bodyguard," she said. "If my publisher finds out that you're my bodyguard, she'll start asking questions that I don't want to answer."

"What are we going to tell them?" he asked. "I mean, if I'm traveling from town to town with you, won't your publisher become suspicious?" he asked.

"Well, I've thought about that and maybe we could tell her that you're my boyfriend," she squeaked out the word boyfriend and her cheeks turned the cutest shade of pink. Yeah, taking this assignment was going to be a whole lot more fun than he originally thought, and watching Justice squirm was going to be the best part.

103

JUSTICE

J ustice Hanks wasn't sure how she was going to convince Steel to pretend to be her boyfriend, but she had no other options. Sure, she had left out the part about her stalker not only working for her publisher but also being married to the head of the company.

She reported directly to Janine McDermont and her husband was the biggest slimeball in the industry. Everyone knew it— well, except Justice, but she quickly picked up on that fact when the guy stuck his hand down her skirt and said some of the dirtiest things she had ever heard. Devin McDermott was the foulest human she had ever met, and that was saying a lot. Janine had booked her a six-month book tour with a European extension if all went well with the US portion. She was finally living her dream but Devin showing up at her signings wasn't part of the plan.

At first, she thought that Janine had sent him to check up on her at her first signing, but she quickly found out that wasn't the truth when Janine told her that Devin had quit the firm. He had accepted an offer at another publishing house and Janine was livid. She said that she couldn't believe that her husband would betray her that way, and Justice knew that telling her about Devin's other betrayals wouldn't end well for her. How could she kick a woman while she was down? The truth was, she couldn't. The longer she let things go, and the more Devin showed up at her signings, the more she knew that she was in trouble.

He started sending her those disgusting text messages and that's when she started to really worry. The last few were raunchy and suggested that he was going to show up at her home. That was her last safe haven and Justice knew what she had to do. She had to go to Steel, of all people, and ask him for help.

"Wait—you want me to pretend to be your boyfriend?" Steel asked.

"I do," she agreed. "I need my publicist to think that every-thing is going smoothly so that my book tour doesn't get canceled."

"Does she have any idea?" he asked.

"I don't think so," Justice said. "Will you do it?" she asked. "Will you take the job and pretend to be my boyfriend?"

He let out his breath and dropped her hand from his own. She thought for sure that he was going to turn her down. "I'll do it," he said, surprising her. "But you need to talk to your publi-cist. If this guy keeps showing up, it's going to become a prob-lem." He had no idea just how right he was, but the less he knew about her situation, the better. All Steel needed to know was that she had a stalker and he needed to keep her stalker away from her. Justice would have to find a way to handle the rest of it when the time came.

"I'll take care of everything else," she agreed. "Now, I need to get home and hang up a few of the security cameras that I just picked up."

Steel groaned and sat back down behind the crappy folding table that he was using as a desk. His office looked as though it was thrown together with things that he found in his basement. "I'm assuming that he knows where you live?" he asked.

"He does and he's told me that he plans on stopping by. I can't let that happen. My home is my place of refuge. I write there and if he shows up, unwanted, I don't know what I'll do."

"You'll move in with your new boyfriend who already has a great security system in place," Steel drawled.

"I think that you're overestimating my new boyfriend's enthusiasm about our relationship," she teased. Steel threw back his head and laughed and Justice was suddenly transported back to high school, staring at him as though he was the most beautiful boy in the whole world.

"I think that your new boyfriend would be fine with you moving into his place for a while," Steel said.

"Is your place decorated like your office?" she asked, looking around his messy office.

"What's that supposed to mean?" he asked.

"It means, you really don't have much in the way of furniture and my place is cozy. I even have a home office set up as my writing space. If I move into your place, I won't get much writing done and I'm on a deadline," she said. Her publisher had her on a tight deadline and not meeting it wasn't an option.

"Okay, how about if your new boyfriend sets up a real security system at your house and then moves in with you for a while, just to make sure that this creep doesn't show up there?" he asked. She had to think about that one. On one hand, having

Riding Hard

Steel around would give her a sense of security, but on the other hand, he'd be a giant distraction and one that if she wasn't careful could cost Justice her heart again.

"I don't know if that's a good idea," she insisted.

"Listen, you want to hire me to keep you safe. If your stalker knows where you live, I'll need to put in better security measures than just sticking up a few store-bought cameras. At least let me put in a good security system for you, Justice. We can negotiate the rest later." Steel was right—she was hiring him to keep her safe and that meant while she was at home too.

"Fine," she said, "you can come over and put in a security system."

"Great, I'll grab something for us to eat and be over by five," he said. "I just have one client to check in on and then, I'll grab my gear."

"Something to eat?" she asked. "You don't have to get us food, Steel."

"Sure I do," he said. "It's the least I can do to make up for being an ass to you in high school."

"I hate to tell you this, but it's going to take more than one dinner to make up for all of that," she said.

"Noted," Steel said, "and, if you let me move in to keep an eye on you, it will give me more opportunities to make things up to you and clear my good name." Justice couldn't help her giggle as she shook her head at him. One thing she knew about Steel was that he was a smooth talker when he wanted to be. She had noticed him charming his way around town over the past few months that he had been home and joined his brothers' security team. The women all over town were vying to get his eye, but Steel seemed blind to all their efforts.

"I'll consider it," she lied. There was no way that she'd let

Steel move into her home to sweet talk her like he did the general female population in town. No, she had learned her lesson when it came to falling for Steel Blane—the hard way. The one thing she knew about herself after all these years was that she was a quick learner, and second chances were only ways to let people in to hurt her. Justice wouldn't be making that mistake again.

What's releasing next from K.L.? Here's a sneak peek! Be the first to get your hands on Blade's Christmas Ride (A Christmas Novella-Royal Bastards MC: Huntsville, AL Chapter Book 13) coming December 2023!

BLADE

Blade walked into Savage Hell with his sister by his side. He knew that he was going to have to keep a fucking leash on Wrenlee, but that wouldn't be anything new. His sister was never one to behave and bringing her to a bar full of horny bikers might not be his finest decision, but he really had no choice. He needed to get some help with his little sister, and he knew that his brothers would give him a hand.

They walked hand in hand to the bar and he could feel the eyes of every guy in the room staring them down. Most of them were probably thinking that he'd picked up a woman, and he'd let them go on believing that too because there was no way that he'd let anyone approach her, even if she was smiling and flirting with most of the guys at the bar.

"Who's the girl?" Savage asked, looking his sister over. As the club's Prez, Savage made it his business to know every member's business.

Blade leaned in to whisper, "She's my sister," he said.

"Why are you whispering?" Savage loudly whispered back.

"Because I don't want anyone to know that she's my little sister. I'd love to get in and out of here without ever dude in the place hitting on Wren."

"Ah, got you," Savage said. He turned to his sister and flashed his best smile. "Hi, Wren," Savage said. "I'm Savage."

"Oh—you're the one who my brother needs to talk to," she shouted over the bar. Blade groaned and rolled his eyes, causing Savage to laugh. At this point, every guy in the place now knew that the woman standing next to him was his sister and Savage found her funny. She'd have bikers lining up around the corner to ask her out if he wasn't careful.

"How about we go back to my office before your brother pops a vein in his neck?" Savage asked. "He seems a bit worried about you, Wren."

She sighed, "All he ever does is worry about me," she grumbled. "I just want to live my life."

"Maybe if you stopped making the wrong fucking decisions, I could leave you alone to live your life, but you don't seem able to do that, Wren," Blade growled.

"Okay, let's table this fight until we get back to my office," Savage ordered. They followed the big guy back down the dark hallway to his private office. He quickly unlocked the door and held it open for the two of them.

"Oh, my girlfriend, Trixie is coming to meet me here. Can someone tell her where I am?" she asked Savage.

"What the fuck, Wren?" Blade shouted. "You invited Trixie to come here for this? We're here to ask for help to get your ass out of trouble, not to meet up with friends, drink and have a good time."

"You wouldn't know how to have a good time if it hit you in

Riding Hard

the face, Blade," Wren hissed. "For your information, Trixie is the one who needs help, not me."

"Wait, you called me at the break of dawn, crying and telling me that you were in trouble and needed help," Blade reminded. Hearing his phone ring at five in the morning wasn't the most pleasant way to wake up. Hearing his little sister crying and saying that she was in trouble, yet again, surely wasn't the way that he wanted to start his fucking day.

"Well, I told you what you needed to hear to help me. I knew that you wouldn't help Trixie. I mean, you've made it very clear that you hate her." His sister was wrong—dead wrong. He didn't hate one single thing about her oldest childhood best friend. In fact, he fucking loved everything about Trixie, not that he'd ever tell his little sister that.

Wren and Trixie were inseparable growing up. They liked to tell people that they were sisters, which totally fucking confused the hell out of Blade when he started looking at Trixie as more than a kid sister. Hell, she was his fucking walking wet dream.

"Why does your friend need help?" Savage asked, sitting behind his big desk. "And why did you tell Blade that you needed his help?"

Wren sunk into the chair in front of his desk and smiled. "Well, Blade already thinks the worst of me, so it was easy to get him to believe that I was the one who needed his help, so I lied," she said.

"Great," Blade grumbled. "I'm sorry to have wasted your time, man," he said to Savage. "Let's go, Wren." There was no point staying if she didn't need help, but Wren seemed to have other plans.

"I'm not leaving until I find someone to help Trixie. She's my best friend. You've known her practically her whole life, Blade.

Would you so easily turn your back on her?" Wren asked. That wasn't a fair question. She knew him well enough to know that he would end up helping Trixie. Wren was right—he'd known her his whole life and there would be no way that he'd leave her to face trouble on her own.

"What did she do?" Blade asked.

Wren barked out her laugh, "Trixie didn't do anything," she insisted. "We went out two nights ago, to one of the local clubs that we like to go to. We were dancing and this guy approached us and asked Trixie to dance. She told him that she was already dancing with me, and he called us both a few names, saying that we weren't worth his time. He left us alone for the rest of the night, but when we left, we found some of those nasty things that he called us spray painted on Trixie's car."

"How did he know which car was hers?" Savage asked.

"I have no clue," Wren said. "Neither of us went out to the car the whole time we were there. We stayed in the club the whole time." Savage shot Blade a look and he could almost read the guy's mind.

"Which club was it?" Savage asked. "I have lots of friends in this area and can call in a favor to get the video footage. We need to make sure that it's the same guy and not a coincidence."

"It was the Palms Night Club," she said. "We usually go there and have no issues, but this time was another story. It wasn't just her car that was vandalized," she said. "I went back to her place with her for the night. She was going to take me home, but the whole thing really shook her up, so I agreed to spend the night with her at her apartment. When we got there, her front door was open and the same words the guy called us were written in red spray paint on her walls, furniture, just about everything."

Riding Hard

"Do you remember the guy's name?" Blaze asked, sitting down on the chair next to Wren.

"It was Bruce." They all turned to find Trixie standing in the doorway and Wren stood up and crossed the room to hug her.

"I was so worried about you. Why didn't you call me?" Wren asked.

"Because I didn't want you to be involved in this mess any more than you had to be. I mean, it's only a week until Christmas and here I am, ruining everyone's day," Trixie insisted. She was always worrying about everyone but herself. She practically took care of Wren while they were growing up. If it wasn't for Trixie, his sister would have ended up in a lot more trouble than she had while growing up.

"Still, you can't go and disappear on me like that again, got it?" Wren asked. Trixie nodded and Wren ushered her into the room, making introductions between her and Savage.

"Why did you disappear?" Savage asked.

"I already said that I didn't want to bring trouble to Wren," she repeated. "This guy seems to be obsessed with me, and I didn't want her involved."

"Where did you go?" Wren asked.

"I went back home and stayed with my parents, but he showed up there too. I was hoping to stay with them through Christmas, but I just couldn't stick around once he showed up at their house." They had all grown up about half an hour from Huntsville in a little town called Athens.

"You didn't run far then," Blade said.

"No," she breathed, "I didn't. Again, it's almost Christmas and I was hoping to celebrate with my family."

"Wait—I thought that we were going to celebrate together," Wren said.

"I was going to call you in a day or two, after I was sure that I was safe, and ask you to come home." Wren wrinkled her nose and shook her head. He knew that his sister wasn't about to go home to Athens. She hadn't been home since her fiancée had died in that bad truck accident; he had a few years back. She and Lee were high school sweethearts and his death devastated Wren. After his funeral, she moved from Athens to Huntsville, saying that she wanted to be closer to Blade, but he knew that it was just Wren's way of running from her problems.

"I figured that would be your reaction," Trixie said. "That's why I didn't call you."

"You could have at least warned me that you were going home. I stopped by your place last night and was worried when I didn't find you home," she said.

"I hate asking you all for help so close to the holidays, but I have nowhere else to turn," Trixie said.

"You should have turned to us first," Blade said. "I don't have plans for Christmas. I can help," he said. Yeah, he knew what he was getting himself into. Blade was in for a whole lot of nights standing under the cold spray of a shower, but not helping Trixie wasn't an option. He was going to find out who was stalking her, and then, he was going to do his absolute best to keep her safe. Keeping his hands off of her was going to take a fucking Christmas miracle, but he was at least going to try.

TRIXIE

Trixie Hammer wasn't about to turn down the help that Blade was offering, but how was she going to hang out for the holiday with the guy she had a crush on since she was a kid? She couldn't think of a time when she didn't have a thing for Blade, but she lived by the promise she made to his younger sister, and her best friend, that no boy would ever come between the two of them. Trixie had a sinking feeling that falling into bed with Blade would end their lifelong friendship because she wasn't looking for anything long-term. She'd eventually have to walk away from him and Wren and that would break her heart. Wren had been by her side through thick and thin. When Wren's fiancée died suddenly, Trixie practically moved into Wren's apartment with her. That was just how it was between the two of them, except for now. If she let Wren be a part of her life now, she'd end up in just as much trouble as Trixie had found herself in.

She hadn't been completely truthful with Wren when she

told him that she didn't know the guy who had asked her to dance at the club. She knew Bruce Trent very well. He had been stalking her for almost six months now, not that she shared that bit with Wren or her sexy brother.

Trixie had met Bruce at a work mixer that she was forced to attend. She told her boss that she had to get home to feed her cat, but he knew that she didn't have one. He called her bluff and dragged her out to a local pub and bought her way too many mixed drinks. When Bruce asked her to dance that night, she said yes. That was her first mistake. She should have turned him down then too, but she had her beer goggles on, and honestly, he was pretty cute. The problem was, he wasn't Blade, and that had her saying goodnight to him, even after he all but begged her to come back to his place with him. She knew better than to follow a guy home after just one dance; Trixie just had no idea that Bruce would follow her back to her place and try to force him way into her apartment. That was the first time she had called the cops on the guy. It wasn't the last time though, and now she had dragged her best friend into her mess. Sooner or later, she'd have to come clean and tell Wren the truth, but there was no way that she'd be able to admit to being a complete fool in front of Blade.

"I hate to ask you to have to babysit me over Christmas, Blade," she said.

"It really isn't a big deal. You can come to my place. I've got great security and an extra bedroom." She wasn't sure if she pouted when he mentioned an extra bedroom or not. Honestly, she was hoping that he had a little one-bedroom place where she'd have to share his bed with him, but that would be just tempting fate.

"Plus, I'll be able to check in on you if you're over at Blade's

Riding Hard

place," Wren said. Trixie had to admit—seeing her best friend more often would be nice. As it was, they were only hanging out a few times a month now, usually going to clubs and dancing. That wasn't really her scene anymore, even though Wren seemed to love their nights out, Trixie was more of a homebody.

"I'd like that," she said to her friend. Wren took her hand and smiled.

"It's settled then," Wren said. "You'll go with my brother, and he'll take you back to your place to grab a few things. Then, you'll go home with him, and he'll keep you safe."

The big guy sitting behind the desk, whom they called Savage, laughed. "You always this bossy?" he asked Wren.

"No," Wren defended.

"Yes," Blade countered.

Trixie rolled her eyes. "They've been like this for as long as I can remember," she admitted. "I can't tell you how many ties I had to break over the years. And for the record, yes, Wren has always been this bossy."

"You know, you don't have to be on his side just because he's keeping you safe," Wren grumbled.

"I know, I'm just being honest. And I honestly love your bossy ass," Trixie said, pulling her in for a quick hug.

"I love you too," Wren said. As an only child, Wren was the closest thing that Trixie ever had to a sister. The only problem with them being sisters would mean that Blade would be her brother and she had enough impure thoughts about him to make that impossible. No, she'd be fine with Wren being her best friend because at least then, she could fantasize about Blade and the number of beds he had in his house.

"I can tell you that we won't be stopping by your place, Trixie," Blade said. "In fact, we aren't making any stops. I need to

117

make sure that this Bruce guy didn't follow you here and is waiting for your next move. If he knows where you live, and knows where your parents live now, he won't stop trying to find you."

"Oh," Trixie breathed. "You make it sound like I'm going to be trapped at your place."

"You are," Savage said, "you will need to stay there until we can figure out what this guy wants and if he's a threat. I'll do some digging into who he is."

"All right," Trixie stuttered. If Savage researched the guy hard enough, he might find that she actually had met Bruce before the other night. Wren would find out that she had lied to her and that would be a disaster.

"I don't want to put you out," she said to Savage.

"Not at all. Blade is one of our brothers and we help each other out all the time. You seem to be family to him and Wren, so that makes you my family too." Trixie wasn't expecting him to say that. It was sweet that he wanted to help her, but it also meant that she'd have to come clean with Wren sooner than later.

"That's very sweet of you, Savage," Trixie said.

"We better get going," Blade grumbled. "I'm sure that Savage has to get back to the bar. I'll drop you off at your place, Sis," he said.

"Um, I was thinking about sticking around here and having a beer or two," Wren said. Trixie could tell that her friend was egging on her brother, and from the way the vein in Blade's neck seemed to pop out, it was working. Even Savage seemed to be able to tell that Wren was getting under Blade's skin.

"Man, I don't envy you," Savage teased.

"Thanks," Blade grumbled. He turned to Wren and grabbed

Riding Hard

her hand. "You are not staying here with these guys. They'll eat you alive."

"Well, that doesn't sound half bad to me," Wren teased.

"Good fucking Lord," Blade mumbled to himself. "We're leaving." He pulled Wren along with him and she turned back to smile at Savage.

"Good meeting you, Savage," Wren said.

"You too, Wren," Savage said.

"Thank you again for your help," Trixie said.

"No problem," Savage said, "I'll be in touch with Blade as soon as I have some information about your stalker." Yeah, she was going to have to come clean with Wren much sooner than she wanted to, but her friend deserved to hear about her bad decisions from her and not some guy who ran a biker bar.

Blade's Christmas Ride Universal Link-> https://books2read.com/u/bQeqdd

ABOUT K.L. RAMSEY & BE KELLY

Romance Rebel fighting for Happily Ever After!

K. L. Ramsey currently resides in West Virginia (Go Mountaineers!). In her spare time, she likes to read romance novels, go to WVU football games and attend book club (aka-drink wine) with girlfriends. K. L. enjoys writing Contemporary Romance, Erotic Romance, and Sexy Ménage! She loves to write strong, capable women and bossy, hot as hell alphas, who fall ass over tea kettle for them. And of course, her stories always have a happy ending. But wait—there's more!

Somewhere along the writing path, K.L. developed a love of ALL things paranormal (but has a special affinity for shifters <YUM!!>)!! She decided to take a chance and create another persona- BE Kelly- to bring you all of her yummy shifters, seers, and everything paranormal (plus a hefty dash of MC!).

K. L. RAMSEY'S SOCIAL MEDIA

Ramsey's Rebels - K.L. Ramsey's Readers Group
https://www.facebook.com/groups/ramseysrebels

KL Ramsey & BE Kelly's ARC Team
https://www.facebook.com/groups/klramseyandbekellyarcteam

KL Ramsey and BE Kelly's Newsletter
https://mailchi.mp/4e73ed1b04b9/authorklramsey/

KL Ramsey and BE Kelly's Website
https://www.klramsey.com

[f] facebook.com/kl.ramsey.58

[O] instagram.com/itsprivate2

[BB] bookbub.com/profile/k-l-ramsey

[twitter] twitter.com/KLRamsey5

[a] amazon.com/K.L.-Ramsey/e/B0799P6JGJ

BE KELLY'S SOCIAL MEDIA

BE Kelly's Reader's group
https://www.facebook.com/groups/kellsangelsreadersgroup/

facebook.com/be.kelly.564

instagram.com/bekellyparanormalromanceauthor

twitter.com/BEKelly9

bookbub.com/profile/be-kelly

amazon.com/BE-Kelly/e/B081LLD38M

WORKS BY K. L. RAMSEY

The Relinquished Series Box Set

Love Times Infinity

Love's Patient Journey

Love's Design

Love's Promise

Harvest Ridge Series Box Set

Worth the Wait

The Christmas Wedding

Line of Fire

Torn Devotion

Fighting for Justice

Last First Kiss Series Box Set

Theirs to Keep

Theirs to Love

Theirs to Have

Theirs to Take

Second Chance Summer Series

True North

The Wrong Mister Right

Ties That Bind Series

Saving Valentine

Blurred Lines

Dirty Little Secrets

Ties That Bind Box Set

Taken Series

Double Bossed

Double Crossed

Double The Mistletoe

Double Down

Owned

His Secret Submissive

His Reluctant Submissive

His Cougar Submissive

His Nerdy Submissive

His Stubborn Submissive

Owned Series Boxset

Alphas in Uniform

Hellfire

Finding His Destiny

Guilty Until Proven Innocent

Royal Bastards MC

Savage Heat

Whiskey Tango

Can't Fix Cupid

Ratchet's Revenge

Patched for Christmas

Love at First Fight

Dizzy's Desire

Possessing Demon

Mistletoe and Mayhem

Bullseye- Struck by Cupid's Arrow

Legend

Spider

Blade's Christmas Ride

Savage Hell MC Series

Roadkill

REPOssession

Dirty Ryder

Hart's Desire

Axel's Grind

Razor's Edge

Trista's Truth

Thorne's Rose

Lone Star Rangers

Don't Mess With Texas

Sweet Adeline

Dash of Regret

Austin's Starlet

Ranger's Revenge

Heart of Stone

Smokey Bandits MC Series

Aces Wild

Queen of Hearts

Full House

King of Clubs

Joker's Wild

Betting on Blaze

Tirana Brothers (Social Rejects Syndicate

Llir

Altin

Veton

Tirana Brothers Boxset

Dirty Desire Series

Torrid

Clean Sweep

No Limits

Mountain Men Mercenary Series

Eagle Eye

Hacker

Widowmaker

Deadly Sins Syndicate (Mafia Series)

Pride

Envy

Greed

Lust

Wrath

Sloth

Gluttony

Deadly Sins Syndicate Boxset

Forgiven Series

Confession of a Sinner

Confessions of a Saint

Confessions of a Rebel

Chasing Serendipity Series

Kismet

Sealed With a Kiss Series

Kissable

Never Been Kissed

Garo Syndicate Trilogy

Edon

Bekim

Rovena

Garo Syndicate Boxset

Billionaire Boys Club

His Naughty Assistant

His Virgin Assistant

His Nerdy Assistant

His Curvy Assistant

His Bossy Assistant

His Rebellious Assistant

Billionaire Boys Club Six Book Boxset

Grumpy Mountain Men Series

Grizz

Jed

Axel

A Grumpy Mountain Man for Xmas

The Bridezilla Series

Happily Ever After- Almost

Picture Perfect

Haunted Honeymoon for One

Rope 'Em and Ride 'Em Series

Saddle Up

A Cowboy for Christmas

Summer Lovin' Series

Beach Rules

Making Waves

Endless Summer

The Bound Series

Bound by Her Mafia Bosses

Bound by His Mafia Princess

Dirty Riders MC Series

Riding Hard

Riding Dirty

Riding Steel

The Dirty Daddies Series

Doctor Daddy

Baby Daddy

A Princess for Daddy

A Daddy for Christmas

The Kink Club Series

Salacious

Insatiable

WORKS BY BE KELLY (K.L.'S ALTER EGO...)

Reckoning MC Seer Series

Reaper

Tank

Raven

Reckoning MC Series Box Set

Perdition MC Shifter Series

Ringer

Rios

Trace

Perdition 3 Book Box Set

Silver Wolf Shifter Series

Daddy Wolf's Little Seer

Daddy Wolf's Little Captive

Daddy Wolf's Little Star

Rogue Enforcers

Juno

Blaze

Elite Enforcers

A Very Rogue Christmas Novella

One Rogue Turn

Graystone Academy Series

Eden's Playground

Violet's Surrender

Holly's Hope (A Christmas Novella)

Renegades Shifter Series

Pandora's Promise

Kinsley's Pact

Leader of the Pack Series

Wren's Pack

Made in United States
North Haven, CT
11 March 2025